THE DERBY MAN IN A HOLE

*They were trapped with one desperate
chance to escape . . .*

With a slow upward lift, he raised Julia. Her weight was less than a hundred and twenty pounds and Darby performed the motion effortlessly.

Darby was filled with pride in the way Julia was handling herself. Already she was at least twenty-five feet up.

That's when he heard the sound of scraping tin from high above.

"Nice try down there," floated a mocking voice. "Sorry."

At the surface, the ladder was yanked away from the wall and slammed over to the opposite side. Wood splintered and Julia dropped screaming as Darby lifted his arms and braced himself for the impact.

Her momentum buckled his legs until his knees struck rock.

From up above, laughter rippled down as the tin scraped across the hole, blotting out daylight like an eclipse of the sun.

*For the first time,
Darby Buckingham thought of death.*

Bantam Books by Gary McCarthy

THE PONY EXPRESS WAR
SILVER SHOT

Silver Shot

Gary McCarthy

BANTAM BOOKS
TORONTO · NEW YORK · LONDON

SILVER SHOT
A Bantam Book / January 1981

ISBN 0-553-14477-4

Published simultaneously in the United States and Canada

Bantam Books are published by Bantam Books, Inc. Its trademark, consisting of the words "Bantam Books" and the por-
trayal of a bantam, is Registered in U.S. Patent and Trademark
Office and in other countries. Marca Registrada. Bantam
Books, Inc., 666 Fifth Avenue, New York, New York 10103.

For Marilyn Best,
good Nevada friend

ONE

The heavy crunch of rolling ore wagons, the staccato popping of bullwhips, and the unending banter of drunken Virginia City miners filtered up from C Street but were ignored by the famous dime novelist. Darby Buckingham was deeply engrossed in putting down the final lines of his latest and best western novel, *The Pony Express War*.

As he penned the last sentences, Darby felt the rich sense of contentment and satisfaction that came to him only with the completion of a story well told. With a flourish, he wrote THE END and eased back in his chair. Wait, he thought happily, until his New York publisher, J. Franklin Warner, reads this one! Darby felt quite justified in allowing himself a rest and, for a few weeks at least, he would do nothing but lounge about, sip his favorite brandy, and enjoy that fresh shipment of Cuban cigars.

Yes, he needed time to increase his weight back to a respectable 255 pounds and rebuild his enormous strength up to the level of his circus strong man days. Darby flexed his right arm, tested its hardness. Not bad. From his desk drawer, he produced a tape measure and wrapped it around his mighty bicep. He was down only a quarter of an inch from his top form and was confident his personal weight-lifting program would soon negate the small loss.

Darby liked to eat, drink, and smoke his expensive cigars—and he even enjoyed testing his strength by hoisting whatever seemed challenging. But most of all,

1

he liked to relax and think—think of his work and of Dolly Beavers, whom he would soon ask to come for a visit to help him wile away the hours with her exuberant charms. But not quite yet. Not until he had a chance to rest and regenerate his energies.

He was just about to pour himself a brandy and launch into reverie when he became aware that a violent quarrel was taking place in the street below.

"Conrad Trent! We know you're inside. Open the door and come out. We have to talk to you. It can't wait any longer."

Darby frowned, and tried to ignore the angry distraction that lifted upward.

"Look out, he's got a gun!"

"Hold it, driver! Move for that rifle and you're asking for trouble."

"I got him covered!"

"Mr. Trent. You owe us our mine back. We found it and it's ours!"

Darby Buckingham forgot about his drink and moved to the window. Everyone on the Comstock knew of Conrad Trent. Some said he was a saint and others thought he was the devil. In the few days that Darby had been in town, he'd heard the man's name whispered a dozen times and it never failed to create heated controversy. Now, Darby had the chance to see this Trent fellow and judge for himself the nature of the man. And, since he was in Virginia City to create another story, Conrad Trent might just have enough color to be useful.

"Mr. Trent, we don't want to come in after you, but so help me God we will. Open up!"

Darby brushed aside the curtains and poked his head out the window. In the middle of the street, he saw an ornate carriage, resplendent with silver fittings and gold handles, an impressive show of wealth made even more striking by a huge team of muscled sorrels whose coats shone like polished brass.

The source of the trouble was instantly apparent. A disreputable-looking fellow had grabbed the lead horse's bit and was struggling for control. His two young friends stood almost below Darby's window with poised rifles, angrily summoning Mr. Trent to disembark. All three appeared to be unwashed rabble, and Darby noticed they were very nervous, in contrast to the carriage driver who looked down upon the trio with contempt and, almost, anticipation. The driver had the lines in one hand but, in the other, a menacing blacksnake dangled into the street. He looked capable of using it at any moment.

The two riflemen seemed unsure. Both were young and either they had never felt the sun on their cheeks or else they were very scared, because their faces were white and bloodless.

"Mr. Trent. We just want our mine back." A long silence was broken by a cracked voice. "Mr. Trent, if you don't come out, we'll have to start shooting. We don't want it that way. Sir, you're leaving us precious little choice."

The silence grew taut as hundreds of onlookers waited with expectancy. One old man ventured a step out of the mob of onlookers. "Quinn Cassidy, you and your kid brother better turn and run while you've still got time. You're fixin' to get yourselves killed!"

There was a general murmur of agreement all around and the Cassidy brothers glanced worriedly at each other. Darby could almost smell their fear. Even from a distance of sixty feet, he could see how violently their rifle barrels quivered.

The lead horse was fighting for its head and starting to rear in its traces as the miner up front struggled to keep the animal under control. "Quinn," he called, "I can't hang onto this beast much longer!"

Quinn swallowed, then aimed his old muzzle-loader at the curtained window. "I'm going to count to five, Mr. Trent. Five is all, sir. Don't make me shoot."

The young man glanced around, saw the growing crowd of spectators and blinked the sweat of fear out of his eyes. "What are you all staring at!" he screamed.

No one answered. Most looked away.

"Why don't you go about your business instead of

standing around gawking?" Still no answer. From Darby's vantage point he could tell that young Quinn Cassidy was very near breaking.

"Every one of you is afraid to speak out against the likes of Conrad Trent. But he didn't slick you outa a fortune like he did us. It ain't fair! All we're asking is to get our mine back. He ain't put one dollar of his own into our claim. It . . . it just ain't fair what he did and he ain't going to get away with it this time!"

Quinn cocked back the hammer and began to count. If he'd expected any sympathy or support, he now realized it wasn't coming. "One." A long pause. "Two."

Darby's sausage-thick fingers tightened down hard on the window frame when he saw the far-side carriage door begin to inch its way open.

"Three."

"Quinn Cassidy! You're making a big mistake."

The harsh warning bulled its way through the drawn curtains and muffled the count of four. "Listen carefully. I'm going to allow you exactly five minutes to get off the Comstock. If you aren't heading down this mountain by that time, I'll see you're buried proper in the morning."

Quinn's brother turned and Darby could see the wildness in the kid's eyes. He couldn't be more than thirteen and Darby watched him grab his older brother by the sleeve and whisper something urgent. Darby didn't have to read his lips to know the boy wanted to run.

"No," Quinn shouted harshly, "it's ours, not his! We've got to stand together, Patrick!"

Quinn straightened his thin and already work-stooped shoulders. On the off-side of the carriage, the door swung further outward.

"Listen to your kid brother and live to send wages back to Ireland," Conrad Trent ordered. "You've just four minutes left."

Darby leaned forward until his upper body was completely out the window. He couldn't explain it, but he had a dead certain feeling that the three young Irish miners were going to die.

The fools! It was like watching a tragedy unfold from the balcony seats of a theater. He wanted to shout a warning that a man was sneaking out of the carriage door. Maybe the fellow holding the team was supposed to guard against this very maneuver, but now all of his energies were concentrated on the fractious horse.

Darby saw a hat brim slide along the rooftop and knew what was going to happen.

"Quinn Cassidy," the voice from behind the curtains purred, "I want you to listen very carefully to what . . ."

Darby whirled and raced to his closet. He threw open the door and groped inside until his fingers closed on his ever-faithful double barreled shotgun. Why was he getting involved in this trouble! Hadn't he just gotten out of enough dangerous situations while working on *The Pony Express War?* Virginia City was a violent town and with every day that passed at least one man was shot to his death in some kind of quarrel.

He hesitated at the closet door. "Stay out of it, Buckingham," he growled.

The voice, so cool and reassuring, drifted in through his window. "Quinn," it soothed, "you're a good lad and you just had some bad luck. Run fast while there's still a chance for you and Patrick and Dave to live."

The voice. It was almost hypnotic. Resonant, reasonable, and yet—somehow deadly. The writer yanked his shotgun up and checked to make certain it was loaded. He wasn't going to use it, of course. This was none of his affair. Maybe the young trio's claims were totally unfounded. That was entirely possible. Or perhaps they'd been foolish enough to gamble away their new discovery and had decided to take it back at the point of a gun.

Darby snapped the breech of the shotgun closed and pivoted towards the window. He wasn't sure what he could do but at least he had to try and stop a senseless killing. Maybe he could cover everyone from his window until a peaceful solution could be found. Maybe . . .

"Quinn, look out!"

It was Patrick's voice. High and shrill like a terrified child. The warning was instantly pierced by gunfire.

Darby lunged for the window and yanked his rifle up, taking off a hunk of paint and wood.

The Cassidy brothers were on the ground and either dead or wounded while the one who'd been responsible for containing the horses was fleeing down the street. Everyone watched Conrad Trent, resplendent in a perfectly tailored white suit, flick his gun out of its holster.

"Right foot, through the heel!" he called to his staring audience. Then, without even appearing to bother aiming, he fired. Darby's head snapped around and he saw the runner cry and break stride as he pitched headlong into the street and rolled in the dust grappling for his right boot.

The carriage driver slapped his Winchester against his shoulder and took aim at the fallen runner.

Overhead, Darby Buckingham also took aim but at a different target.

"No!" Conrad Trent commanded. "Let him live. Roan, I'm ordering you not to fire."

Darby gratefully eased the killing pressure off his trigger, knowing full well that, from this distance, he'd have peppered the street and maybe hit innocent bystanders. Roan obeyed, but argued vehemently—first, to kill, then just to horsewhip them until this day's lesson was written on their backsides.

"He's dead!" Patrick wailed, seeming to regain consciousness with a rush. "Quinn is dead!"

"It's his fault," Trent said dispassionately. He was a big man, tall, solid, and ruggedly handsome with dark, piercing eyes that seemed to go through the frail, ragged boy at his feet. "If you were a man you'd be dead as well. I don't shoot kids, even though you'd have killed me."

He scanned the silent crowd, then reached into his

pockets and threw some money down at Patrick Cassidy. "That's for the decent burial I promised. After Dave sees the doctor, you both are leaving the Comstock."

Patrick spat on the money, then he spat on the perfectly creased pantleg of Conrad Trent.

Trent's face flamed. He reached down, pulled the boy to his feet, then drew back his fist and knocked him spinning into the dirt.

Someone in the crowd swore and Darby Buckingham cursed so vehemently that Trent looked up at him. Their eyes locked for an instant before the man turned back and addressed what had now become a clearly antagonistic group of witnesses.

"They would have killed me and I had every right to defend my good name. Is there any one of you who would not stand up to defend his own hard-earned reputation? A reputation of trust and confidence."

He lifted his arms dramatically. "Gentlemen, within your midst are plenty whom I have assisted to become prosperous. Yes, prosperous!"

"Not all of us, that's for damn sure!" an apron-wearing saloon keeper griped.

Darby saw a quick flick of anger rise on Conrad Trent's cheeks as he whirled to confront his detractor.

"Who said that!"

The speaker appeared to melt in stature and refused to identify himself.

Trent's face muscles relaxed and he laughed outright. "I know it was you, Jess Arnold. Come on, stand up tall and let those around you benefit from your mistakes."

Someone pushed Arnold to the fore and other men snickered at his quaking knees.

Trent did not seem to notice, but now appeared to be enjoying himself. "Jess, is it not true, when I doubled your stock, I then strongly advised you to sell at a profit? And did I not also demonstrate my conviction by divesting myself of that very same stock?"

Arnold's head bounced up and down like a cork on

a fishing line. He wouldn't even meet Trent's eyes.
Darby grunted with disgust. What a spineless excuse
for a man!

Conrad Trent radiated righteous vindication. "There
you have it. One more pitiable accusation set straight."
His eyes scolded them all, then he smiled. "Gentlemen,
I have, by my own reliable sources, just received some
very valuable information relating to the stock market.
And now I am about to take action based upon that
information, and place several orders by telegraph to
the San Francisco Stock Board. As a demonstration of
my integrity, I am going to invite . . ."

Darby failed to catch the rest of the words. All eyes
were on Conrad Trent like an actor on center stage.
But Darby witnessed something else. He saw young
Patrick Cassidy's thin fingers inching towards his rifle
—very, very slowly.

Darby choked back a warning as the thought struck
him that Conrad Trent might very well use the time
advantage as an excuse to kill the young Irishman. The
writer pivoted and raced for his door. There was only
one way to prevent another brutal killing and that was
to reach Patrick before he could get his hands on that
rifle. Darby barreled down the plushly carpeted hallway of Virginia City's finest hotel and leapt to the
stairway, taking the steps three at a bound. He detested moving quickly; his short, thick legs were built
for power, not speed. Yet, as he rushed down into the
lobby, the image of those fingers spidering toward the
rifle propelled him on. He would snatch the weapon
out of reach before the young fool created the opportunity for his own demise. Then, then, by God he'd
have a word or two for Mr. Conrad Trent! The man
had obviously convinced the others that he'd reacted
purely out of self-defense, but Darby disagreed. The
trio seemed to be no more than scared kids begging for
a hearing.

One thing was clear as Darby stormed across the
lobby—if he was any judge of character at all, then the
high and mighty Mr. Trent was an egocentric, spell-

binding rattlesnake. In booting the defenseless Patrick, he'd earned Darby's lasting contempt.

The loud crack of rifle fire told Darby he was too late. Yet, even as he slammed through the doorway, he heard another sound. Not gunfire, but a sharp, popping noise. Darby collided with a spectator and knocked the man sideways as they both flew headlong into the street.

When he looked up, he realized the carriage driver called Roan was going to demonstrate the fine art of using a bullwhip. Darby saw Conrad Trent stoop to retrieve his ivory stetson from the dust, then poke a finger through a bullet hole in the brim. For a moment, everything seemed to hang suspended as the crowd's eyes were glued on the stockbroker. Then Conrad Trent ran his manicured fingers through his thick shock of silver-dusted hair and his chin dipped. Once.

That was all the signal Roan needed. The whip slashed across twenty feet of ground and bit the flesh out of Patrick Cassidy. It was so savage that Darby blinked before he roared with anger as his own voice joined Patrick's cry.

He'd left his shotgun upstairs realizing it would only result in more death, and he was unwilling to let himself be drawn into a crossfire between Conrad Trent, his driver, and the man who'd slipped out of the carriage unnoticed. Now, as he hurtled forward, he wished he'd brought the shotgun. Even before he'd traveled six feet, Roan had already snapped the whip again and was about to do so once more.

The quickness of arm and wrist drove the whip with unbelievable speed. It appeared to be at least twenty feet long, braided leather with a thick wooden handle.

"Stop!" Darby bellowed, trying to prevent even more damage.

Roan's eyes widened as he saw the big man coming in at a labored run. He probably had four seconds before Darby's outstretched hands could reach his throat—he needed less than two. Roan's weight piv-

oted on line and the whip retreated behind, then his
wrist and arm pumped forward and the blacksnake's
metal-tipped fang came toward Darby Buckingham.

Instinctively the dime novelist threw up a forearm to
protect his eyes. The whip snaked across his lower legs
and brought him crashing to the dirt. Even before he
could recover, he heard the blacksnake whisper again
and retreat.

"You'd better go for my throat," Darby rasped,
"because I'm going for yours!"

"Come on, then!" Roan challenged. "Get up, big
man, and I'll teach you how to mind your own business. Git!"

Darby was half erect, crouched and gathering himself to spring, when the whip flicked out and drove at
his face. He twisted and tried to block its path but the
metal tip slid by his arm and bit him over the ear.

He grabbed for it—but missed and wanted to shout
with frustration.

"Come on!" Roan goaded, almost dancing with ea-
gerness and blood-lust.

Darby charged with his arms up as protection. He
heard Roan's laughter, then saw him maneuver sideways, shaking out the blacksnake just the way he
wanted before throwing it to bite. The snake came in
low again, intent on wrapping itself around his legs and
tripping him down once more.

He bent and made a grab for the whip and was
instantly sorry for the mistake. It was like gripping a
fiery stick and it paralyzed his left hand.

Darby's breath was coming faster and he knew he
was in no shape for this. Each time he charged he was
slower, while Roan was barely exerting himself. It
would only get worse unless he somehow changed the
tide. As it was now, he had the feeling that Roan was
just waiting for him to drop his hands and grab for the
whip—that's when it *would* go for his throat.

Lying in the dust, feeling warm blood trickle down
from the wound over his ear, hearing the crowd shout
with excitement, and watching Roan make the whip

behind him move like an expectant sidewinder, Darby had an idea. Not a brilliant one, but a desperate one. He had to maneuver Roan up against something so the man couldn't draw back the whip and send it forward.

Roan was standing ten paces in front of the lead carriage horse. Darby climbed to his feet and began to position himself for what he frantically hoped was his last charge.

"Come on, Mister. Quit trying to circle in on me!"

Darby's lips curled and he continued around just out of range. Now, he had the man's back to the horses. If he could just get close enough to make Roan retreat a few steps. Maybe the whip would get fouled under the horse's feet, maybe . . .

Maybe he was a fool. Roan was too clever to allow himself to be backed up close to an entanglement—twenty years of practice too clever.

Darby saw the man glance over his shoulder then begin to sidestep his way clear. There was nothing left now but to charge.

He threw his right forearm up before his face and kept his other bloodied hand low and outstretched. The blacksnake came flying in at his knees. Fast. Nothing more than a blur and a hum. It struck and wrapped as Darby threw his legs apart and grabbed for leather. His hand was wet and, for a moment, he thought the whip was going to slip free to strike again.

But it didn't. It slid across his palm until the metal tip caught on his ring and then Darby's hand closed down tightly. He wanted to laugh when he saw Roan's face. Gone was the man's sneer and now he struggled desperately to pull free.

Darby made a quick circular motion, wrapping the leather around both hands, and then he gave the whip a brutal yank. The result was like snapping a carp out of its pond. Roan completely left the ground and hurled forward with his arms extended and still gripping his whip's handle.

When he flopped to earth, Darby pounced on him.

He reached down and dug his fingers into the man's throat and, like an enraged bear, began to shake Roan senseless. Only an iron will and his last pain-filled bit of reason kept the ex-circus strong man from collapsing his victim's windpipe.

Only that—and the gun barrel that cracked against his skull.

When Darby awoke, he was surprised to find himself outstretched on a magnificent 18th-century Louis XVI chaise. The carpet upon which he gazed was of a rich Persian pattern, and an ornate crystal and silver chandelier glittered from the ceiling.

"Good evening, Mr. Darby Buckingham."

He sat up fast, too fast. For a moment, Darby thought his head was going to split with pain. He groaned, gingerly touched his scalp.

"It's a nasty one, all right. But Doctor Parker says you'll be fit again in a day or two."

Darby nodded. "What am I doing in *your* house, Conrad Trent?"

The man gave a short bark of laughter. He was dressed in a pale, seagreen smoking jacket and had a drink in one hand and a very fine smelling cigar in the other. "I volunteered my services until you are feeling better, Mr. Buckingham."

"Why?" Darby asked roughly. "Unless the entire experience I just endured was a bad dream, then *you* are the cause of my rather severe headache."

"Oh, come now!" Trent protested, showing the most perfect set of teeth Darby had ever seen. "You really can't accuse me of causing that ridiculous bit of trouble. I was just trying to reach my office. Besides, I didn't know until afterward it was you."

Darby forced himself to sit up and felt a moment's dizziness. He was in no mood to banter with Conrad Trent. Not now. Not ever. "Did you hit me?" he asked, looking up quickly.

"Why, of course not!" An almost hurt expression came to the man's eyes.

"Then it was your other man. What's his name?"

Trent frowned with disapproval. "Let me pour you a drink, Mr. Buckingham, before we talk."

Darby's flash of anger nearly drove him back to the supine position as a bolt of pain seared across his forehead.

Trent mistook his groan for an acceptance and, while Darby massaged his head between his palms, he heard the clink of decanter and glass.

"Drink up, Mr. Buckingham! This first is to your health and . . . wealth."

Darby's glass never quite reached his lips. "Is that why you didn't try to run me out of town like the Cassidys?"

"What do you mean?"

"I mean," Darby said levelly, "my wealth!"

"Oh, that." Trent waved the suggestion aside. "Well, one *expects* a gentleman such as yourself to be of independent means. But no. That's not why you're here."

Darby was certain that was *exactly* why he was being hosted. Yet, the whiskey was excellent and he had some questions on his mind that needed answering. "Tell me about the Cassidy brothers."

"What's to tell? I'd rather discuss other things." He smiled warmly and said, "You know, I was pretty excited when I discovered you'd taken up residence in Virginia City."

"You were?"

"Sure!" Trent boomed. "By God, man, you have no idea how much we've got in common."

"You're right," Darby answered cryptically. He couldn't imagine what he and Conrad Trent would have to share—except, perhaps, their ability to afford luxury.

Trent walked up close and was about to lay his hand on the writer's shoulder when something in Darby's eyes made him think better of the idea. "Let me explain."

"Please do."

Trent shifted his broad shoulders, took a pose, and began, "To start with, you're one of the finest men ever to step into a boxing ring. I saw you beat the hell out of Terrance Kilpatrick in Boston, John Reynolds in New York City, and I even went clear to Philadelphia to see you take out Rocco Perez in twenty-seven rounds!"

"How interesting," Darby said without enthusiasm.

Trent doubled his fists together and his eyes were shining. "Interesting isn't the word for it, Mr. Buckingham—more like unforgettable. By God!" he cried, driving an uppercut into an imaginary opponent then flicking out his left hand and dancing away, "you were a boomer!"

Darby finished his drink. It was time to leave. He was proud of his ring career but it was too personal for sharing with this polished stranger. Besides, there were a couple of fights he'd just as soon forget—like the one when he shattered Dennis Foster's jaw, giving the poor man a disfigurement to bear the rest of his life.

"Don't go yet!"

It wasn't an order, more of a plea, and that was startling coming from Conrad Trent. The man dropped his fists. "I guess you don't want to talk about those days?"

"That's right."

"I understand. But you must also understand that I was just a kid and you were my hero."

Darby bristled. A kid! He'd be blasted if Conrad Trent was any more than five years his junior.

"You're the reason I took up boxing in college. Undefeated, you know," he quipped, trying to make it sound light but not quite succeeding.

"I should have guessed," Darby rumbled.

Conrad Trent smiled. "I'd almost enjoy going a few rounds with you now."

Keep it up, Darby thought, and you will.

"But then, as you can see, I've kept myself in remarkably good trim and you ... well," he smiled, "you've sort of . . ."

"Sort of what!" Darby breathed, coming to his feet.

By the angels in heaven, he'd had almost enough of this pompous, posturing peacock!

"Oh, nothing," Trent said, a devilish glint in his eye. "Let's change the subject. I can see I'm upsetting you, and Doctor Parker said you should keep quiet."

"To hell with the man! Do you want to go a round or two?" Darby's blood was up and he was ready.

"It wouldn't be fair!"

"Of course it wouldn't," he conceded, "but it was your suggestion."

"My error then," Trent said apologetically. "Maybe sometime when you're feeling better."

Darby's breath exploded from his lungs, why the . . .

Conrad Trent had wisely turned with the pretext of selecting a cigar for Darby. "Cubans, sir. I'm sure you'll enjoy the smoke."

Darby stared at the cigar. "It's all I do smoke," he said testily.

Trent smiled and this time his teeth reminded Darby of rows of perfectly chiseled little white tombstones. "See there, we've got things in common I never even realized."

"I've got to be leaving, Trent. But, before I do, I insist on some kind of explanation about those Cassidy brothers."

"What the eye doth see and the heart doth feel, oh, so often, is totally unreal."

Darby blinked in confusion as the man waited. And waited.

Trent stayed silent until it became apparent he was not going to receive a response of any kind. "It's mine," he said happily. "I *wrote* that for my fourth book of poetry. So that's the other thing we have in common. We're both writers."

"Writers!"

"Yes. Of course," Trent said, his voice quite serious, "even you wouldn't pretend that your sensationalist dime novels are anything approaching art or the poetic form, but . . ."

Darby felt the heat rise into his cheeks. "Say it again," he gritted.

"Pleased and honored. It does seem to be profound if I do say so myself. What the eye doth see and the heart doth feel, oh, so often, is totally unreal."

"*You're* unreal!" Darby roared. "And your so-called poetry is nothing but doggerel! Tripe! Rubbish!"

Conrad Trent's mouth went slack. He backpedaled as though he'd been struck. But he recovered quickly. Gone was the role of a gracious host and, in its place, a hard and determined twist shaped his lips. "Why, you hack!" he spat. "You run-of-the-mill hack! I ought to . . ."

Darby Buckingham heard no more. He took three short strides across the expensive rug and grabbed Conrad Trent by the lapels of his seagreen smoking jacket and slammed him up against the wall so his feet couldn't touch the floor.

"Before I take your head off," he panted, "I want to know about those Irish boys. I want to know the truth. Now!"

Trent was over six feet tall and heavy enough to indicate plenty of muscle. But at that moment, he was helpless.

"Let me down, Mr. Buckingham, and I'll get the gloves and we can . . ."

"Blast the gloves! What about the Cassidys!"

"First let me down, sir!"

Darby had to admire Conrad Trent's aplomb. Most men would have squirmed like a rabbit, but this one only glared menacingly. He let Trent down.

The man straightened his jacket and seemed to weigh throwing a punch before deciding not to. "All right," he said angrily, "the Cassidys are nothing but stupid Irish trash who got lucky, then greedy."

"Go on."

"They hit promising dirt and came to me for a loan to develop their claim. I convinced them to incorporate and issue shares."

"Why?"

"Because that's the way everyone operates on the Comstock. You issue shares of stock and invest it in the mine. People buy those shares with the expectation of becoming millionaires. Some actually do."

"What went wrong?"

Trent shrugged, studied his fingernails. "At first, the stock did very well. Well enough that Quinn got to thinking they should issue more. He was like an ignorant child who thought all he had to do was make paper money. I warned him not to do it."

"Why?"

Trent muffled a phony yawn designed to indicate the question reflected so much naivete as to bore him. Darby recognized his gesture and wadded up the man's jacket in one hand and drew back his fist. Trent instantly dropped his condescending attitude.

"Because I knew our . . . their stock would plummet," he gasped. "With my business experience I know that when you issue more shares it makes people think the mine isn't as sound as they'd first thought."

Darby wrenched his hand free. "Then what happened?"

"They wouldn't listen! We had words and I kicked them out of my office." Trent's eyes blazed. "Can you imagine those kind of people telling me *my* business?"

"Never mind that. Finish your story."

"With satisfaction," Trent said in a clipped voice. "Their stock went to hell. Dropped to almost nothing. Creditors began to descend on them and they lost the mine."

Darby shook his head. The story wasn't what he'd expected. Though the writer knew very little about mining stocks, Trent's account seemed reasonable. An uneducated immigrant would make that kind of error.

He scowled and decided to leave before he slapped that arrogant grin off Trent's handsome face.

At the door, he was halted by the metallic cocking sound of a pistol.

"That's far enough, Buckingham."

Darby expelled the air from his lungs and wondered why he'd shown mercy only a few seconds earlier.

"Turn around."

Darby followed orders. How could Trent have gotten a pistol so quickly? He hadn't even heard so much as the scraping of holster leather.

"I'm going to tell you the 'afterward' part of this story because you'll hear it anyway. I saw what was going to happen and, when it did, I bought almost all of those mine shares for little or nothing."

"So, you own the mine now." It was a statement, not a question.

"As much of it as I could buy on the market. Nearly seventy-five percent. Perhaps you should think of this as a lesson to heed in the future. Conrad Trent *always* wins. Fists, guns, or just plain wits. But I'm no blood-lusting murderer. I'll only kill if threatened or cornered. Remember that."

"I'll remember," Darby answered. "And you can be sure I'm going to find young Patrick Cassidy and hear the other wide of that story."

He hurled his cigar to the floor and ground it into the Persian rug. Maybe he ought to switch brands. It was the *only* thing he and Conrad Trent had in common.

The man stared at the rug and the pistol shook in his fist. "That Cassidy boy is gone from the Comstock. Probably back to Ireland and his mother. Forget about him! But, as for us, we'll have another time, Buckingham, though I'd advise you to avoid it as long as possible. Even hack writers have a purpose."

Darby used every ounce of his self control and then some. This was not the place nor the time. Sooner or later though, it *would* come. Of that, he was dead certain.

TWO

Dolly Beavers felt her heart begin to palpitate as she hurried away from the Postmaster's Office toward the hotel which she owned. The Antelope Hotel was the finest lodging house in Running Springs, Wyoming, and, as Dolly made her way down the boardwalk, she was greeted with respect by the town's leading businessmen. Ordinarily she would have stopped to chat, perhaps even flirt a bit with several of her handsomer peers, but not today. Today, her eyes were shining with expectation and it was because of the letter in her gloved hand.

Darby Buckingham's letter.

Men bowed or doffed their hats as she moved down the boardwalk and, for once, she scarcely noticed the frank looks of admiration or the way their eyes followed her.

Dolly Beavers was a vibrant and sensual-looking woman. Her figure was one of deliciously defined curves and she had a way of smiling at men that could leave even a riverboat gambler off-balance and unnerved. Her lips were a promise; her eyes seemed to have the quality of shining blue magnets. And, when Dolly spoke, there was a natural smokiness to her voice that said here was a man's woman. Her hair was long and golden and her walk, while not being consciously practiced, was highly stimulating and maybe even provocative.

Across the street, lounging before their Great Whiskey Palace Saloon, Bear Timberly and Zack Woolsey watched her with unconcealed enjoyment. Bear Timberly stuck his two forefingers into his tangle of beard and whistled mightily. The shrill noise momentarily penetrated Dolly's happy thoughts concerning the letter and her Darby Buckingham. She saw the pair grinning broadly and her first instinct was to hurry on by. But she was too late in making that clear and her hesitation was all they needed to launch themselves across the street.

"Damn!" she whispered, knowing the letter would have to wait until she could manage to excuse herself. And with this pair, getting free would not be easy. Zack and Bear considered themselves her self-appointed suitors and guardians. More than once, she'd told them she loved Darby Buckingham and they'd be happier pursuing someone else. At this, both men would laugh in big guffaws and tell her it was only a matter of time until she "saw the white light" and came around to choosing one or the other for marrying.

Zack Woolsey swept off his hat and bowed until his face was just inches from the walk; the gesture was remarkable, considering he was at least six and a half feet tall and no longer young.

Not to be outdone, his brother in mayhem whipped off his own coonskin cap and dropped it to the ground. Then, before she could quite believe her eyes, Bear Timberly, his great, thick shoulders dipping, bent down and snatched it up with a click of his tobacco-stained teeth. Yet, as he straightened, they all heard his back pop ominously.

Bear, halfway erect and with the coonskin dangling from his mouth, assumed a stricken look around the eyes. The coonskin fell from his mouth and he gasped, "Uhhh—no! My back. I done splintered my spine!"

Zack roared with laughter, but Dolly shot him an expression that jelled his laughter into a choking gurgle.

"Bear!" she swore, "when are you going to start acting your natural age? You and Zack are too old to be carrying on like this!"

"Help me, Dolly," he pleaded, "I did it for you."

She sighed with resignation. Leaving the man all doubled up like a bent pin wasn't her nature. She'd have to take him upstairs to her room and, somehow, straighten him out.

"You get a letter from Darby?" Without waiting for her answer, Zack slapped his buckskin breeches and his long, deeply creased face became all smiles. "It's about time! We've been gettin' us mad at him for not writin' sooner."

"What's this 'us' business," she demanded. "The letter is addressed to *me*."

"Well now, girl, you know how Darby feels about the three of us. We're like his brothers and you ... well, you're kinda like his little sister."

"Sister!" Dolly's eyes flashed. "That's the last thing he'd call me."

She was mad now. Stomping mad. Couldn't these two old long-in-the-tooth retired buffalo hunters understand she loved Darby? They needed a lesson and she'd give it to them so that, this time, there'd be no misunderstanding.

"The letter is to *me,* not you. And I'll tell you something else. Without even opening it, I know it contains Darby's plea that I come to visit him in Virginia City. Yes, he will beg *me,* not you, to come."

"Beg!" Zack snorted angrily, "when are you going to realize that Darby ain't the kind of man to beg anyone for anything. He's probably doing just fine all by his lonesome."

"Impossible. He needs a woman and ..."

"There'd be plenty of 'em in Virginia City. None as pretty as you, but where there's gold there's always women."

Her cheeks were aflame. How dare this man suggest that her Darby would ... the thought was so abhorrent she couldn't even think about it.

"Dolly, my back is killing me!"

"We best get him up to your room and try to get him upright," Zack said. "He looks to be in real pain. Maybe hearing from *our* good friend in Nevada will perk him up some."

Dolly glared at the bent-over figure. Her gloved fists knotted and she wished she wasn't a lady so she could straighten both him and Zack up. But good.

"Miss Beavers!" Bear grimaced, his face at waist level. "The letter. You're crumpling it up."

Dolly unclenched her hand but the damage was already done. "I can flatten it back out," she gritted. "Come on, I want to see your faces when he writes asking me to catch the first stage to Virginia City."

Dear Miss Beavers:

I must begin with my sincerest apologies for not having written sooner. Since arriving in Virginia City, I have been daily occupied with becoming acquainted with the fascinating history and personalities of the Comstock.

Perhaps, in a few brief lines, I can detail how this fabulous Bonanza came to be discovered, as well as the current description and state of affairs I'm witnessing in my research.

To begin is to start in early 1859 where the Comstock was discovered by an irascible blowhard by the name of Henry Comstock, although everyone here refers to his memory as Old Pancake because, it is said, he was too lazy to bake bread and consumed his flour in the nature of Pancakes. He shared this discovery with another crusty miner named Old Virginny who, having gotten roaring drunk one night, crashed to earth shattering his bottle of whiskey. As the story goes, he was so mortified by his comrade's laughter, he drew himself erect and solemnly proclaimed, 'I hereby christen this mountain Virginny, after myself.' And the name stuck. Now Virginia City is a mecca for seekers of fortunes.

I'm also told that there were two young Irishmen, Patrick McLaughlin and Peter O'Riley, who were in on the strike a few miles farther north but were bluffed into forfeiting major shares of their claims by Mr. Comstock. Whatever the truth may be, it was interesting to me to learn that these first discoverers were greatly distressed by a peculiar "blue stuff" which clogged their rockers and made their *arms ache from tossing it away. Six months later, the troublesome "blue stuff" was found to be almost pure silver mixed with gold, assaying at an unbelievable $3,876 per ton!*

Word was not long in reaching the thousands of idle miners in California whose fortunes had greatly declined since Marshall's Forty-Niner discovery a decade earlier.

Today, the entire Comstock is an anthill of activity and industry. The first arrivals tried to placer mine the ore, a procedure that had been so successful in the California Mother Lode. Now, it is apparent that the ore in Sun Mountain runs broad and deep. Each week, huge new pieces of machinery are freighted in to make the extraction possible. They go ever deeper and find seemingly inexhaustible bodies of ore.

The city itself is nothing which might be called permanent, though every day new buildings seem to rise from the ground. Most of them are saloons.

This is the most barren and inhospitable land imaginable and there is little in the way of greenery. As far as the eye can see, the runty pinion pine and juniper trees have been chopped off for firewood or for underground shoring purposes.

Virginia City, although an aesthetic wasteland, is rife with silver fever, but I'm told the price of extraction will become very costly in human lives. The miners, many of whom are from Cornwall, Wales and Ireland, take a fearful death loss. Cave-ins are commonplace and, to relieve their monotonous and brutal existence, these men drink hard. Killings occur almost daily.

Despite all these things, I am excited about my coming stay and feel a sense of real anticipation. The people are colorful and ever ready to tell a story. They are a cross section the likes of which has never been assembled on one rock-strewn mountaintop. All are making high wages but spending it almost as fast as it comes. The barkeeps and prostitutes get most of it and one Madame, a woman named Julia Bulette, is so popular she has been honored by having a fire company named after her. After accidentally meet-

ing Miss Julia, I can see why. She is a raven-haired beauty and is very charming. Had I not already been forewarned of her profession, I would never have guessed. Miss Julia has already consented to allow me to include her in my next story—a story that is only now beginning to unfold in the eye of history.

It is my opinion that the most astounding discoveries are yet to be made. Great fortunes will surely be realized by those stouthearted and daring enough to uncover new riches or trade wisely in a spiraling stock market.

Next letter, I will tell you about my encounter with Virginia City's most prominent stock investor, a man named Conrad Trent. You will find the account interesting at the very least. I must go now. I have a research appointment on this afternoon's calendar with the infamous Miss Julia for background research.

Please relate my news to Bear and Zack and rest assured, dear woman, you are never far from my thoughts.

> *Sincerely,*
> *Darby Buckingham*

Dolly's big china-blue eyes misted and she blinked them rapidly to keep the tears from obscuring her vision. In futile hope, she skipped back over the letter, knowing she hadn't missed a single word and the long-awaited invitation. No. He hadn't sent for her as promised.

Disappointment made her ache inside and the final lines of the correspondence regarding that Julia woman made her heart turn cold and fearful. Why did he bother to mention her? Background research, indeed! Surely he wasn't attracted to that kind? Yet the description aroused deep warnings and a sense of urgency.

Zack cleared his throat. "Miss Dolly," he said, his voice carrying disappointment edged with ill-concealed relief, "It's like I told you. That Buckingham is all wrapped up in his own discoveries and too busy to send for his friends."

"Yeah," Bear offered in his most tactful fashion. "He's more than likely to marry that prostitute woman and forgit all about us."

Dolly's composure broke and she covered her face and bawled. Her sobs weren't small and ladylike but great breast-bursting cries that made Zack and Bear's faces go white with anger. Both men tried to comfort her at once and nearly got into a skirmish.

"Oh, stop it!" she sniffed lustily. Dolly blew her nose and dabbed away her tears while Bear relinquished his headlock on Zack and the room grew quiet.

"Miss Dolly?"

"Yes, Zack."

"Well, ma'am. I guess that there letter spells it out plain enough for all of us. And I don't mean to be rushing you—neither of us does," he added, glancing at Bear and receiving a nod of encouragement. "But with old Darby out of the picture, I reckon it's time you said which one of us you're going to get hitched up to."

Her breath sucked in and her chin jerked up. "Marry you! Why, you heartless scoundrels! Do you dare think for a moment that I'm the kind of woman who gives up so easily?"

They nodded, but without conviction.

"Well, you're wrong!" she cried, leaping to her feet. Dolly Beavers started pacing back and forth and there was nothing provocative at all in the way she moved now. Oh, the grace was still intact, but it was the grace of a stalking mountain lioness.

All at once she halted and looked about, and her lips drew down at the corners. Her ample bosom rose and fell very rapidly and the two old hunters seemed to realize they'd better keep still until whatever was about to happen finally did.

"I'm going to sell out," Dolly pronounced. "Starting today, I'm going to take the first decent offer for this hotel that comes along and I'm moving to Virginia City."

She jabbed a finger in their direction. "Do you want to buy me out? I know you're making good money off the Whiskey Palace in spite of yourselves. How about it?"

They both squirmed. Appeared speechless.

"Well, don't just sit there!" she demanded. "Thanks to Darby Buckingham, who helped you get started two years ago, you're now in the financial position to snatch the finest hotel between San Francisco and St. Louis right from my hands. I am prepared to offer you a deal."

Bear leaned in close to his partner and whispered frantically. Zack growled something unintelligible and batted his partner along the side of the head.

Dolly jumped in between them before they could really start punching. Once they got up their steam, they could destroy a place.

"That's enough! Just a yes or no will do. And, if it's no, then I'll ask you to leave. I've got another buyer in mind and I'll telegraph him this very afternoon."

Zack swallowed loudly. "We don't want to buy your place, Miss Dolly."

"Then . . ."

"Whoa up!" Bear roared. "We'll leave all right, but first you oughta know that the only reason Zack and I have stuck in the saloon business all this time was because of you. Hell! We even change our socks and long underwear once a month on your account. If you leave, none of this . . . this respectability that's chafin' our shoulders accounts for nothin'. Don't you realize that, Miss Dolly? We . . . we love you."

Dolly blinked, swallowed noisily. For the second time that afternoon, her eyes brimmed and now she felt deeply ashamed of herself. With her voice trembling, Dolly raised her arms until they were outstretched. "Come here," she said with a faint catch in her voice.

They did. Both men grabbed her in a hug and she drew their rough old heads to her tear-streaked cheeks.

"Boys," she whispered. "We've all got a problem. I love Darby and you love me and there isn't any of it working out right. But I tell you one thing and that's that we've got to stick together."

They nodded, too overwhelmed for words.

"So, if you're willing, and with the Lord's own good help, I'm going to sell both our places and we'll all go away together."

The next few moments were pandemonium. Zack and Bear went crazy with happiness. Half laughing and half blubbering, they told her how deathly sick of running a saloon they'd become. They wanted adventure, not the rocking chair. They both swore that, for the first time in two years, they could feel their old blood pounding again.

"We'll pool our money," Dolly promised, "and we'll get Darby to help us strike it rich on the Comstock."

"We can't lose!" Zack bellowed. "Together, we'll make a fortune."

Dolly nodded enthusiastically. When they became rich, she'd buy the loveliest dresses in San Francisco and a grand house with servants. Then how would that lowdown Julia stack up? And maybe she'd show that Darby Buckingham a thing or two about being jealous. The Comstock was a man's world and she'd have those handsome bachelor millionaires falling all over themselves trying to court her favor.

Yes, she thought, up to now she'd done it all wrong. Darby had grown too damned complacent about their romance. He needed the spur of jealousy to realize he'd better marry her—or lose her.

Dolly Beavers could hardly wait to get started.

"Who's the buyer, Miss Dolly?"

The image of a jealous Darby Buckingham faded away, as did her knowing smile. "He's a Laramie banker," she said. "The man has bunches of money and wants to expand his investments."

"Will he be looking for a saloon?" Bear asked worriedly. "You know those bankers are pretty uppity about keeping their reputations sober."

It was a sound observation, but Dolly pushed aside

her doubts and said, "We're partners. If he wants the Antelope Hotel like he says he does, then he'll also have to take The Great Whiskey Palace."

They erupted in huge smiles.

"And, furthermore, I think I know a way to get top dollar."

Upon hearing this, the two old moss-backs actually broke into a wild jig as Dolly clapped and laughed.

Now, she thought, if only I can do it.

Dolly was dressed to the hilt. She had purposely chosen the red satin gown with the most daring neckline she owned. And now, with her make-up freshly applied, her long blond hair brushed to a high luster and her best French perfume filling the air, she was ready. No man under eighty-five could possibly resist her charms, and Mr. George Sandopolis was far below that age.

In spite of her preparations and all the care she'd taken to be at her most attractive, when the soft knock at her door sounded, Dolly Beavers was nervous. Mr. Sandopolis was no fool and, during his last visit through Running Springs on his way to Salt Lake City, she'd gotten the distinct impression that he was more interested in acquiring *her* than the hotel. But still, there was hope. To find another wealthy buyer might take a long time and Dolly was eager to strike a bargain at any cost. Almost any, she corrected.

So, as the knock repeated, Dolly nudged the neckline of her dress as low as she dared and waltzed across the room to open the door.

"Why, Mr. Sandopolis," she breathed, "what a pleasure! I hadn't realized your stage had arrived."

His dark eyes glittered as he removed his bowler and, with an exaggerated flourish, swept it to his chest and bowed. He held that pose so long that, before he straightened, Dolly had ample time to study every contour on his bald head.

"Miss Beavers!" he gushed, popping erect in an almost martinet fashion. "You look stunning!"

While his eyes devoured her, Dolly pretended to

look flustered. It was obvious that Mr. Sandopolis hadn't changed in the short months since he'd last visually disrobed her.

She fell back coyly, her senses acute for the battle which would soon begin. Meeting alone in her room with the man was taking a fearful risk but, in case of emergency, Zack and Bear were poised in wait next door with their ears pressed tightly to the paper-thin walls. One shriek or the slightest creak of the bed-springs and they'd come *through* the wall. Mr. Sandopolis didn't realize his own health was in far greater jeopardy than her honor.

"Would you like a drink?" she offered.

His eyebrows raised and he tweeked the tips of his moustache. "I would, indeed, though I must confess the drink I would most prefer would be that of the nectar of your lips!"

Dolly heard an angry grunt through the wall, then a muffled curse.

Sandopolis glanced sideways but Dolly stepped between. "Come over to my liquor cabinet and show me what you'd prefer," she said lightly while taking his arm. The banker, with a final questioning look at the wall, dutifully followed.

Dolly sat rigidly in her only chair and was afraid the small, dark man was getting prepared to leap at her. They'd had three drinks each and, each time, she'd practically had to dodge her way back to her chair. In the next room, things were getting out of hand and she knew she had to get the conversation focused on business while there was still time.

"Mr. Sandopolis . . ." she began.

"George, please."

"All right, George. Well, George, ahh, as I wrote, I'm interested in selling the Antelope Hotel and you did tell me you were in the market for new ventures."

"Oh yes, my dear," he said evenly. "I always antici-pate new beginnings, new adventures. If you know what I mean?"

Darn right she knew what he meant; yet, she pre-tended not to and pushed on stubbornly. "I own, as you know, the best hotel in Wyoming. Twenty-two rooms, all well-furnished. I invite you to examine them and am confident you'll see that $10,000 is a very reasonable price. Very reasonable."

He straightened and, for the first time since they'd come together, his eyes seemed to focus without probing her skin. "Ten thousand, you say?"

"Yes. Not a cent less."

He swirled his cognac thoughtfully. "Perhaps," he said quietly, "we can discuss this matter later tonight after dinner. It would give me time to . . ."

"No!" she blurted and was instantly sorry. "I mean, business before pleasure. Isn't that the saying you men-of-the-world like to use?"

His smile was a little slower in coming but apparently he was mollified. "Yes," he sighed, "business before pleasure. But . . ."

"What?"

"My dear, one without the other is like a sparkling crystal glass without wine. Do you understand?"

She nodded.

"Good, then let's get this business part over with quickly so that we will have more time for the pleasure."

"Yes, let's do that. I'd like to settle this now and get to the bank before closing time."

"Very well," he commented. "To begin with, I do not need to inspect the premises. I've stayed here every time I've traveled to the Mormon capital, as have my business associates. We all concur that you have a fine, well-cared for establishment with charm and taste."

Her spirits soared! "Thank you!"

"For what? Telling you what all of Wyoming already knows? That's nothing. The important thing that everyone also knows is that *you* are the most delicious, beautiful woman in these parts. *That's* why you've prospered." He clapped his hands together in anticipation. "And *that* is what my colleagues also agree."

Dolly wasn't sure whether to nod or deny the statement. And before she could decide, he was talking again.

"I'll pay your price, Miss Beavers, with pleasure."
He winked. "But, on one condition."

She could guess that condition and it set her mind to
racing.

"The condition is that you must remain in my employ."

"What?"

"Yes. You must continue to run this establishment
just as you have in the past. Also," he said with a
knowing smile, "I like to keep close watch on my
investments and so would insist on having my own
room. The one next door would be fine."

"I see," she whispered. The rat wanted her for his
on-call mistress! The very nerve!

Dolly made her face appear composed but it felt like
cracked ice. She pretended to consider the idea.
"There's one more thing, Mr. Sandopolis. I have an
interest in the Great Whiskey Palace across the street.
I should like to see the two sold together."

He scowled and she could almost see the wheels of
his mind turning. "I'll buy anything if the price is right
and the, ah, rewards are satisfying enough. How
much?"

"Twenty thousand," she said, blank-faced.

"Twenty thousand! That's ridiculous! The place isn't
worth more than fifteen. Why those two old, broken-
down . . ."

He didn't finish because a fist plunged through her
wall and started making grabbing motions. Before the
banker could come to his feet, Dolly had reached the
hand and, unable to think of anything else, she bit it.

A howl exploded in on them.

"What on earth is going on!" Sandopolis raged.

"Nothing. Nothing at all. Don't worry, I'll have it
repaired and I'll move those crazies out so it will
become your room!"

He still didn't look satisfied.

"Tell you what. Buy both establishments and I'll
have a connecting door built where the hole is." She
came into his arms. "You'd like that, wouldn't you,
George?"

She was too much for him. He tried to kiss her but she buried her chin against his neck and whispered a husky endearment. And then, when he attempted to pin her against the wall, she ducked under his arms and retreated to the door.

"First business, *then* pleasure," she cooed.

He charged after her and pursued her all the way to the Bank of Running Springs, never aware that Zack and Bear were not far behind. It was a very near thing, but they just got into the bank by closing time.

Mr. Sandopolis, dry mouthed and scarcely able to contain his passion, quickly ordered the transaction to its conclusion and nearly pushed Dolly through the door before she could count the thirty thousand dollars. He was greatly dismayed when, upon setting his foot outside, he was instantly separated from Dolly by her new partners.

He shouted, ranted, and wailed, but it was no use. When his stagecoach resumed its schedule west toward Salt Lake City and beyond, Mr. Sandopolis was not on the passenger list. But Dolly, Bear, and Zack were.

Clearly, for the Laramie banker, it was going to be business *without* pleasure.

THREE

Darby eased down into his waiting bathtub and sighed with unabashed satisfaction. In one hand he grasped a tumbler of imported brandy and in the other, his cigar. Nothing could be finer; Buckingham was the picture of health and contentment. Yet, he felt he deserved this small reward for the excellent job of interviewing he'd done these past few days. His notebook was evidence enough that he'd been hard at work gathering research on the Comstock. Within its rapidly filling pages were stories of fires, gunfights, cave-ins, and fortunes made and lost in the same day. But that was the way of life in Virginia City; everything changed daily and one could almost feel the air charged with the expectation of a gold and silver bonanza. Here, men worked hard, played hard, drank fast, and died young. No one thought about next year—only about next week or next month when they'd strike it rich.

Darby took a sip of brandy and closed his eyes as the warm water made him drowsy. Soon, he thought, he must begin his book. All he lacked were a few more pieces of information, then he would have to choose a single event or personality around which to build his story. Conrad Trent, of course, would fit as the villain and the game of stock speculation might prove interesting to his western readers. He'd write about how everyone, from the seamstresses to the hard rock miners themselves, bought tremendous amounts of stock by the process of margining. It was craziness, but they purchased twice what they could afford. This was possible because the stockbrokers would advance half the necessary funds and charge the buyer a hefty two percent a month interest on the loan in addition to a one percent commission on all sales and buys. If the stock went up, everything was fine but, if it went down, the city would almost go into public mourning. And each daring soul who'd margined his pay to a lending stockbroker would have to suddenly come up with enough extra money, or "mud" as they called it, to cover his advance, taking into account the falling price of the stock. This they'd do to the bitter end, even if it meant pawning their boots or giving up whiskey. If the stock kept dropping, the poor speculator would be hounded to the ground and forced to come up with even more money to make his broker safe. Usually, at this point, the speculator ran out of "mud" and the broker sold him out, leaving the man nothing.

It was a high-stakes game they played, but few men or women failed to make good their debts. To do so was to lose both credit and respect without which no one, rich or poor, could survive on the harsh Comstock.

The knock on his door made the writer spill his brandy and jolted him out of his thoughts. "Go away," he roared, "I'm in the bathtub!"

Wild laughter erupted in the hallway. Then, just as Darby was closing his eyes again, Zack Woolsey and Bear Timberly executed their famous mountain-man charge, bringing the door in along with them.

"Surprise!" Dolly screamed. "Surprise!"

The cigar in his mouth sizzled to soapy extinction. "What . . . what are you doing here!" he spluttered. "And my door . . . you're . . . carrying it!"

Bear grinned sheepishly, tossed the door onto the bed. "Goddamn," he breathed, "just like old times!"

Before Darby could phrase the reply in mind Dolly was nestled up against the tub, smothering him with kisses. "Oh, Darby, honey! Were you surprised?"

She looked into his shocked eyes. "Yes, I can see you were." Dolly leaned over the bathtub rim and wound her powerful arms about his neck. When she jerked him closer, he slipped in the tub and went under water.

Darby came up fighting and choking with bath water as well as righteous indignation.

"Blast!" he gasped. "Have I no right to my privacy?"

Three broad smiles did a slow fade out and then were replaced by looks of amazement and hurt.

It was Zack who recovered first and he rallied with a vengeance. "Privacy! We pulled up stakes and traveled halfway across the frontier to visit and all you can do is complain about privacy? Damn your privacy, Mr. Buckingham!"

The soapy water made his eyes sting but not as much as the accusing expressions he saw reflected on their faces. Darby cleared his throat. The shock was wearing off and he knew he'd reacted badly. A stranger stopped in the hallway and peered in at them. Darby plucked his floating cigar up and hurled it at the man. "Go about your business, you fool," he bellowed, lifting menacingly out of the water. The onlooker retreated and Darby sank back.

"Now," he said, motioning to Bear Timberly, "would you kindly replace the door and tell me what brought all of you to Virginia City?"

"Oh Darby, how can you ask such a question!" Dolly wailed. "We came to stay and to become Comstock millionaires like you wrote about."

"But . . . but what about your businesses? The Antelope Hotel and the Great Whiskey Palace?"

At this, the trio grinned conspiratorially and told him about Mr. George Sandopolis.

Darby wasn't smiling with them when the account ended. "Miss Beavers," he accused, "you duped the man."

Dolly recoiled. "Would you have preferred that I had agreed to his terms?" she asked in a clipped voice.

She had him there. "No, but it seems to me that you purposely misled him . . ."

"Now, jest a danged minute," Zack warned, stepping up to the tub and glaring down with threatening eyes.

"Yeah!" Bear seconded, "I don't like the way you are acting. I thought we was friends!"

"And I thought you loved me," Dolly whispered, fighting back tears of hurt.

"I do! We are, but . . ."

"But what?" they all yelled.

"Why did you sell! There's nothing here for you. Go back to Running Springs. This is a rough town."

"Are you saying we ain't men enough to take care of ourselves and Miss Dolly?" Bear rumbled.

"No. I'm only saying that all the good mining claims have long since been taken."

"Then we'll buy someone out," Dolly said stubbornly.

For the first time, Darby chuckled. "That's impossible. Top claims on the stock market are selling by the thousands of dollars a running foot. Even if you had a claim, you'd have to hire a ten- or fifteen-man crew to help you sink the shaft. For that you need mechanics, carpenters, engineers, and deep rock miners; their wages could add up to over two thousand dollars a month."

"We could dig it ourselves," Bear spat. "We're tough."

"Sure you are," Darby replied, "but tough enough to go through solid rock for two or three hundred feet?"

There was a long silence. Darby shook his head. "I thought I wrote that this isn't placer mining—it's big business and even I would have difficulty raising enough money to go far underground."

Dolly bit her lip but she also reached into her handbag and pulled out what appeared to be his crumpled letter. She opened it up and scanned over the first few pages until she found what she wanted. Then, with a trembling voice, she read it back to him. "You say here that great fortunes are yet to be realized by those stouthearted and daring enough to uncover new riches or trade wisely in a spiraling stock market."

"I wrote that?"

"You did. Now, are you prepared to tell us you lied?"

"No!" he shouted, slamming his fist into the water. "I've never lied. Perhaps ... perhaps, I got a little carried away with the narrative, but I didn't lie."

She glanced at her partners and Darby felt like an accused man on trial for his life. He couldn't believe this was taking place. "Dolly," he pleaded, "this is your Derby Man here."

But even that failed to thaw the ice in her blue eyes and he saw a steel in her he'd never even suspected. "We're *going* to make our fortune," she said, as her partners nodded solemnly. "And if working a claim is too rich for our blood, then we'll do some of that stock trading you wrote about."

"But you don't know anything about mining," he pleaded.

"We'll learn," Bear promised.

"That's right," she added. "How much does it cost?"

"Not much. But that's not the point! I can't let you throw your money away dealing in stocks you know nothing about. You're my friends."

Dolly's expression softened. For a moment, he guessed she was going to revert back to the sweet, lovable woman he'd known in Running Springs.

But Zack Woolsey came between them. "Don't sell us short, Darby. We're a lot slicker than we might look. Who do we talk to about these stocks or whatever?"

"How should I know? Everyone in Virginia buys and sells them."

"Never mind," Dolly said quietly. She sniffled and her eyes were shining wet as she turned toward the door. "We already know who's the most prominent stockbroker in Virginia City."

"Who?"

She glanced at the letter, then balled it up in her gloved fist and threw it at him. As she went out the door, he heard her say, "Conrad Trent."

"No!" Darby yelled. He *had* to warn her that Trent
was the last man in Virginia City to whom she should
entrust her funds. But, as he started to rise from the
tub, Zack and Bear grabbed its sides and turned it over
on him. His warning was drowned out and, as he
struggled to lift the tub for air, Bear tossed the door on
him. Fortunately, the tub contained his furious oaths.

In the days that followed, Darby often thought
about apologizing for his hasty reaction to having his
door dismantled. Perhaps, if that had been all of it, he
would have. But two things prevented him. One, he
detested apologies and wasn't even sure he could properly give one and two, he was hoping that Dolly would
apologize first. It was always so much nicer when the
other person made the first overture, because then you
could be very gracious about accepting it and feel quite
satisfied you'd been right all the while.

The problem was that Dolly, Bear, and Zack seemed
to have no intention of even speaking to him, much
less apologizing. They'd taken rooms in this very same
hotel but passed him like a leper when he appeared.
That's what made him the angriest. Angry enough to
let them become involved in their own little game and
be taught an expensive lesson. But not too expensive.
Darby had no idea how much money they'd managed
to unload their businesses for, but he certainly didn't
want to see them swindled out of everything. And so,
from his window, he spied on the trio as they bustled
about town and seemed to talk to everyone they met.
Darby was certain of one thing—if he saw them asso-
ciating with Conrad Trent, he was going to step in fast;
that man had all the instincts of an eel and he was
twice as slippery.

Meanwhile, Darby had other concerns and chief
among them was to determine the whereabouts of
young Patrick Cassidy. He didn't believe for a moment
that the Irish boy had fled the Comstock, because
there'd been too much defiance in him to run. It
seemed far more likely that Trent had lied to protect
himself. But from what? That was the question. Darby

had asked everyone he could think of about the Cassidy brothers' mine, which he learned they called The Emerald, and their relationship with Trent. Most people confirmed the stockbroker's account of the matter. Quinn had acted foolishly by issuing too many shares of stock in the promising but still unproductive Emerald. No one seemed to have kept any of the stock and Darby was sure that Conrad Trent had bought it all for the price of a song.

The more the writer thought about it, the more he became convinced that Trent had swindled a fortune out of the immigrants and now was only waiting for the chance to cash in on his maneuvering and trickery. And in the back of Darby's mind was one other question besides the whereabouts of the Irish lad—Trent had rashly admitted to owning only seventy-five percent of the Emerald stock—where was the missing quarter share that figured to be so valuable?

"Blast," he muttered, throwing down his quill pen and leaving his desk. "How's a man to concentrate on writing while fretting about a strong-minded woman and a half-grown boy who's lost both his older brother and gold mine?"

Darby glanced at the empty page beside which lay a stack of rough and scribbled notes about the Comstock. He still didn't have a story, not one he could focus in on and that contained the element of danger and mystery to which his readers were so accustomed.

Then it clicked. Blazed into focus like waking up to black midnight and then striking a match to a kerosene lamp. *This* was his story. Backdropped by towering Sun Mountain and powered by the hum of activity that surrounded it all, a real flesh and blood story was unfolding. But was it enough? Its eventual outcome really affected only the life of one small boy. Or did it?

Darby jumped up and began to pace about. No, he decided, whatever Conrad Trent was up to might well affect hundreds of others in some malign and as yet undetermined way. And no matter what the outcome, Darby was very sure that he and Conrad Trent were

locked into some contest that only time would reveal.
Yes, this was the thread of story that would stitch all
the power and drama of the Comstock together.

Darby smiled, riffled a finger under his black moustache. Once again, he was the main participant in his
account of history. All he had to do was begin the
search for Patrick Cassidy and let the word get back to
Trent. That would make something happen. He'd bet
his life on it.

The Eastern dime novelist grabbed his derby hat
and started for the door. Momentarily forgotten were
the empty pages on his desktop. Ahead lay danger and
a story only he could tell.

Conrad Trent's head jerked up from the ledger when
the knock sounded. Then he forgot about the interrup-
tion and returned to his figures. It was too late for
business callers. They could return tomorrow.

The knock became louder.

Roan looked over quickly. "You expecting company
this late, boss?"

Trent finished adding up the day's receipts and
glanced irritably at the offending doorway. "At this
hour, I expect nothing but aggravation. Honorable men
do not prowl about after midnight."

The third man in the room nodded, then pulled his
gun out of its holster and slid it under the paper he'd
been reading. "Want me to answer?"

"No," Trent said, closing the ledger and locking it
safely into his desk. He slipped the key into his vest
pocket and felt the air of distrust spring up in the
room. To hell with them. Leroy Thomas and Roan had
no idea of the extent of his dealings and they never
would, lest they become greedy.

The knock sounded even louder and Trent, putting
the derringer in his vest pocket, started toward the
door and yelled, "Who is it?"

"Allen Walker," came the high-pitched reply. "I've
got valuable information."

The three men relaxed. Almost smiled.

"More fish to fry," Leroy said.

"We'll see."

Allen Walker's hands were ink-stained, and across his forehead there seemed to be a perpetual indentation where his bank teller's visor left its impression. His round face was still pimpled, though he was in his mid-twenties. Bitten fingernails and a nervous habit of smoothing his thin, sandy moustache gave evidence of his insecurities. The moment Trent had first seen the bank assistant, he'd sensed weakness and greed. Subsequent meetings had proven that first feelings are worth noting and Trent had exploited his discovery.

"Good evening, Sir, I . . ." He glanced fearfully at Trent's companions. They made him nervous. "Maybe I should come by some other time?"

"No, no, it's all right. Come in out of the cold." Trent wasted no time in idle conversation. He didn't like Walker; the bank assistant was a frail excuse of a man. "What's your information this time?"

Walker swallowed noisily and cleared his throat. "Well sir, it's big. Real big."

Conrad Trent decided to pour Allen Walker a drink. It would loosen the kid up and maybe put some color in that sallow skin that was so unhealthy and offensive to look at.

He mixed drinks and, handing one to the bank employee, said, "Give me the man's name."

"It's a partnership, I think."

Trent scowled. It was always more difficult to persuade more than one individual.

"Go on."

"You're going to like this, Mr. Trent. There's two old buffalo hunters who can barely spell their names. Look like they've been living with the Indians all their lives. They deposited twenty thousand dollars."

Trent's expression didn't change. "That'll make it harder. Them not knowing about stocks or even able to read."

"Oh, they can read a little! But I haven't told you the best part yet."

"Then do it."

Walker gulped at his drink. "It's the third one you're going to like. She's . . . well, sir, she's a looker." Walker giggled and, somehow, it was an obscenity.

This time, Trent's voice betrayed him and he spoke too quickly. "Go on, don't stop. Is she married to one of the others?"

"No, sir! Her name is Dolly Beavers and, as far as I can tell by asking, she's a friend of that writer fella."

"Buckingham? Are you sure!"

Allen Walker shrank back from the excitement in Trent's voice. "Yes. That's the one. Apparently, she came to stay with him and they got into an argument."

Trent rubbed his hands together briskly. "How much has she deposited?"

"Well, they're equal partners. That's the way they wanted it and that's how I set things up. They deposited thirty thousand dollars altogether. Said they were looking to cash in and make their fortune here."

"Good work!" He looked up quickly. "You didn't mention my name, did you?"

"Oh no, sir!"

"Excellent." Without asking, he poured everyone in the room a glass of whiskey. Allen Walker didn't seem nervous any more and both Leroy Thomas and Roan acted almost friendly.

"Now," Trent said, "I need some specifics. Who seemed in charge?"

"The woman. No question about that. The other two were falling all over themselves to agree with her. What she says goes."

"Hmmm," Trent mused. "If they're that taken with her, it's going to be hard to deal with. Where are they staying?"

"Starbuck Hotel. Same as the writer."

"Where are they from?"

"Running Springs, Wyoming. At least that's what she put down on their application to deposit."

"Do you know anything about stocks or mining?" He raised his hand abruptly. "Think before you answer, Allen, and if you don't know, then be honest. We can find out."

"Well," he hesitated, "I'm not sure, Mr. Trent. But my guess is that they don't."

"Why?"

"On their way out, I wished them bonanza, not borrasca."

"And?"

"Their faces went blank. They didn't know that bonanza means luck and borrasca the opposite. There's not a miner east of the Rocky Mountains who hasn't heard those terms."

Trent nodded in agreement. "How old is the woman?"

"Thirties. Pretty face. Long blond hair and figure to make you drool. I watched them go back to the hotel and the whole street did like me. I tell you, Mr. Trent, even without her ten thousand you'd be interested."

Something made Conrad Trent ask one more question. "You sound plenty interested in the woman yourself. Am I right?"

Walker's face blazed red. "I . . ."

"Oh, come now," Trent persisted, "be truthful."

"Well," the young man stammered, "if Miss Dolly Beavers was the kind, she could run Julia Bulette herself out of business, and I'd help her to do it."

Trent laughed. "Well put! I'll see how good a judge of virtue you are. Now," he said, lowering his voice, "we operate the usual way. Not a mention of my name—only about Leroy being a geologist. The *only real* geologist on the Comstock. Talk him up good."

"I understand."

Trent led him to the door. "Which will it be this time? Money or a tip on the market?"

Walker played nervously with his sparse moustache. "Sir, this . . . this is a little bigger than most I've told you about. And . . ."

Trent stepped in close enough to smell the man's breath and see the lines in his bloodshot eyes dilate. "Are you going to try and squeeze me?" he whispered.

"No . . . no sir!" Walker swore, backing into the wall. "I just thought, if everything goes the way it usually does, that you might give me a little extra. But . . ."

"Never mind," Trent stepped back and his smile radiated outward. "You've earned something additional this time."

He reached inside for his wallet and peeled out two hundred dollars, saying, "First thing in the morning, borrow whatever other money you can and come by my office. When you get here, make a big show of wanting Emerald Mine stock. There's still a few shares floating around, though I've quietly bought up most of it."

"But, Mr. Trent," he protested, "that stuff is worthless. You said so yourself!"

"Young man, I said I own most of that stock now. Do you really think it will stay at twenty dollars a share?"

"No, but . . ."

"Buy whatever you can and then, when it reaches one-fifty, get rid of it fast."

Walker nodded. "How much can I buy? If you have it all . . ."

"I'll be selling. Slowly at first, then faster as the price soars."

"I see."

"No, you don't. But, if you follow my instructions, you'll do quite well."

"Yes, sir! I'll see you in the morning."

Trent opened the door and let him outside.

"Walker!" he said harshly.

The bank assistant spun around and, when he saw the gun in Trent's hand, he dropped the money and his face went slack with fear.

"If you say one word about me being behind the sudden increase in Emerald's stock value or that I'm planning to dump part of it at one-fifty, then I'll send Roan over to visit you." He sighed deeply. "And that would be very, very unfortunate."

Trent pivoted on his heel and went inside. His last glimpse of Allen Walker had been enough. It wasn't that cold in the night air but the bank assistant seemed frozen, totally incapable of moving even to retrieve his money. The man was going to remember the warning. No doubt about that.

"Well," Roan said, "are you going to handle it the same as always?"

Trent looked at Leroy Thomas. He valued the man's advice though he never let it show. "What do you think, Leroy? See any problems?"

Leroy Thomas was quiet for a moment. He was a handsome man, but not nearly so good looking that people remembered his face. At forty, he already had a comfortable bulge around the waistline and the false impression of success that many working-class miners associated with it.

"No," Leroy said, "it should work as well as usual." A trace of cynicism slipped through. "I assume, once you've insulted and exposed me as a fraud, that I am to make the proper connections so that you can begin unloading part of the Emerald stock. By the way, how much will you sell?"

"Almost half. I'll retain control, though I want to have enough out to create a buying spree. If anyone knew I own most of that stock, the whole charade would collapse. Now, are there any other problems?"

"Just one I can think of. What if Darby Bucking-ham told them about you?"

Trent laughed. "If we play our parts well enough, that shouldn't matter. I'll have this Dolly Beavers woman eating out of my hand in gratitude after our little altercation."

"One thing, Conrad."

"What?"

"Don't punch me so hard tomorrow. The last time, I damn near lost my teeth."

There was no humor in the warning and the stock-broker knew it. He had delivered a perfect blow to his partner's jaw, and it had felt good to realize he could still hit that solidly using his timing and strength as in the old days.

"What about Buckingham?" Roan asked, breaking the strained silence. "I've got a score of my own to settle."

"When I say so," Trent warned. "First, I'm going to give that pompous hack a sound lesson in humility. I'm going to break his spirit. In the meantime, it's going to be your job to keep an eye on him. I want to know everything he does."

"What's the matter?" Leroy asked. "Didn't he understand your poetry?"

Trent whirled and, for a moment, he almost lost control and went for his gun. It would have been an even match. Leroy Thomas was damned fast.

"Never mind my poetry," he rasped. "Before this is all over, I'll have his woman and his pride."

"The woman part sounds easy enough, given your talents," Leroy said. "But maybe he don't care so much about her anyway. Then, where does the pride come in?"

Trent grinned broadly. "I told you he was a boxing champion back east, didn't I?"

"Yeah, but . . ."

"The 'was' is the key word. He's lost it all and you can see that by the shape he's in."

"He's still as strong as a horse," Roan grumbled. "I never had a man work me over that way. You go after him, you'd better have something in your hand, Mr. Trent."

But the stockbroker wasn't listening. He'd turned his broad shoulders to the fire and he was looking deep into the flames, thinking of years gone by and a hero he'd once known.

"You know," he said quietly, "that man was really something about fifteen years ago. I studied every move he had and I know them by heart. Later, when I went to college, those moves carried me through my own string of victories. If Buckingham was in his prime today . . . well, I wouldn't get into a ring with him even if I had a gun."

Leroy chuckled. "But, as you say, he isn't in his prime. And so, you want to fight him."

"I've got to," Trent whispered, turning around to face them. His fists knotted and he held them up to the firelight. "I didn't realize it until I saw him again, but now I know I've got to whip him."

"What if he doesn't want to get into the ring?"

"He will. I'll find some way to do it. Pride is the man's weakness. I saw it in his eyes the other night."

It was Roan who spoke next but he chose his words very carefully. "Boss, we got a good thing here. If . . ."

"If what!"

"If he should, you know, get lucky and . . . ah, got you . . ."

"Beat me?" Trent's eyebrows arched and, surprisingly, there was no anger in his voice. "He won't. It isn't important that I whip him fairly. There are ways, though I don't believe I'll need them."

"But just for insurance, huh, Boss?"

"Yeah," Trent laughed. "Besides, I've always said winning is all that counts. Why start playing fair now?"

Later that night, while he lay in bed, Conrad Trent carefully went over his plans once more. In the morning, Allen Walker would create a lot of sudden interest in the Emerald stock. It would be easy enough to start a rumor that the young bank teller, being privy to the intricacies of finance, must have discovered that fresh money was being invested in the abandoned but guarded mine. That would really create a buying surge and probably take the stock up at least to sixty dollars.

Trent decided to wait three more days before sending ore samples in for assaying. Then, he'd have it said the ore was from a new test wall in the Emerald. By then, Dolly Beavers would be ready to entrust her money to him and her thirty thousand would go into Emerald stock, causing it to soar to at least one-fifty. Since he'd bought his stock for almost nothing, he'd make a small fortune.

There was one other fact that not even Leroy knew about, and that was the twenty-five percent of the stock he'd lifted from Quinn Cassidy's body. It was in his safe at this moment. He'd have to have the documents altered in San Francisco. But there wasn't time now and, besides . . .

Trent sat up in his bed. "Buckingham," he whispered out loud, "I told him! Told him I bought it all except twenty-five percent."

He swore furiously, remembering their almost forgotten conversation. Buckingham might start wondering about that missing twenty-five percent and that would raise questions. Questions he didn't want the writer to go around asking. Trent made himself relax. All right, in a flash of anger, he'd made a serious blunder. But would it really matter? Of course not! Inside a week, it would be past and too late for the writer to interfere. Besides, the fool knew nothing of stocks. The Eastern dime novelist wouldn't be able to unravel the complex scheme.

"Yes, everything fit. The only weak link in his chain was telling Buckingham he'd bought only three-quarters of the stock. All that was available. Conrad decided he'd better work fast to goad Buckingham into the fighting ring. There, he'd humiliate the writer, punch his body and spirit with such a fine display of pugalism that everyone on the Comstock would consider Buckingham an object of ridicule.

Conrad Trent drifted off to sleep with a smile on his lips. Funny how easily a young man's heroes turned to dust.

FOUR

By the time Darby Buckingham finished his usual two-beefsteak breakfast, he knew all about the sudden interest in Emerald stock. The news was on everyone's lips and Darby overheard a man saying that the value of shares had doubled in less than two hours this very morning. No one quite understood why, and many whom Darby questioned didn't care. All that mattered was that something had occurred to raise interest dramatically in the unworked Emerald mine and that was enough. Buy, they all said, when a stock began to sour and you couldn't go wrong unless you hung on into its downswing.

The writer left the restaurant in a hurry. There was no doubt in his mind that Conrad Trent stood to gain most from this morning's events. And it was a tragedy that young Quinn Cassidy hadn't waited another week before facing up to Trent. If he had, he'd have been worth a lot of money. Now, all that remained was his younger brother, Patrick.

The evening before, the writer had learned that the Irish boy was working in the Consolidated Mine, although no one could recall seeing his face in Virginia City after his brother was shot. Darby didn't waste time renting a carriage. The Consolidated was one of the biggest companies on the hill and less than a mile from town. Its great buildings and ore tailings spilled over at least two acres and the mine ran twenty-four hours a day.

He was puffing from exertion in the thin mountain

air by the time he reached the main office. Stepping inside, he identified himself at once to the superintendent, a brawny man of about fifty, with red hair and a wide, square-jawed grin.

"Mr. McKenna, I'm here to see a boy by the name of Patrick Cassidy."

The grin faded. "Why?"

"It's a matter of great urgency. It has to do with the Emerald stocks."

McKenna studied him carefully, seemed to be considering Darby's intent. "You look to me like you might be a friend of Conrad Trent," he said finally. "And if you are, then . . ."

Darby scowled and wasted no time in telling the superintendent what he thought about Conrad Trent. He also mentioned that he was the one—the only one—among a whole street full of spectators, who'd come to the aid of Patrick and Quinn Cassidy.

McKenna listened, then beckoned Darby to a seat in his private office. "I heard about that and I'm proud to meet you. Patrick Cassidy is a good boy and, though I can't prove it, I think Trent deliberately misled them into losing the Emerald."

"But if we *could* prove it, then. . . ."

"You can't," McKenna snapped. "I've talked to the boy and he admits no one forced them to issue too much stock. There is just no way of proving what Trent's intentions were, though we both know they were dishonest."

"Does Patrick still own any stock?" Darby asked quickly. "If he does, then at least we could salvage that much."

McKenna frowned thoughtfully. "You'll have to ask him, Mr. Buckingham. For whatever it's worth, I don't think the boy owns a single share."

Darby wanted to object, but decided to keep his own thoughts quiet. He'd find out soon enough. "What makes you say that?"

"You're not going to like this. I don't myself, but the kid won't listen to reason. He insists on staying down in the mine."

Darby leapt from his chair. "You mean all the time!"

"Take it easy! I told you I don't approve, yet he seems to feel his life is in danger if he's seen in Virginia City."

"But . . ."

"There's something else," McKenna cautioned, "the reason I don't think he kept any stock is that he's begging me to work double shifts."

"A thirteen-year-old boy! That's criminal!"

"Sure it is," McKenna growled, "but what can I do? Say I refuse, and make him leave. Then, if he gets killed, it's on my conscience. And even if Trent lets him be, Patrick would just go to work for someone else during his free time. No doubt at much lower wages."

Darby threw up his hands in futility. "But why?"

"Because, like a whole bunch of other immigrants, his family probably went far into debt to finance the passage over from Ireland for Quinn and young Patrick. There's people going hungry over there, Mr. Buckingham. That makes a boy grow up fast."

"So," Darby graveled cynically, "the family's hopes rest on that poor youngster's shoulders and he's going to kill himself trying to carry an unholy load of responsibility."

"It's not that bad," McKenna argued. "I've taken the boy under my wing, kinda, and so have a lot of the men on his shifts. He's well fed though he works it off, and he's not abused with heavy labor."

"Good," Darby said, not feeling it. "Can I go down and see him? Maybe . . . maybe, if he still has some of those Emerald certificates, all our problems will be solved."

"Could be," McKenna said, but there was no hope in his voice. None at all.

Darby's spirits were at his feet as he and the superintendent trudged toward the giant structure that covered the hoisting works. It was a cold and gray-clouded day, but at least he could feel fresh air on his cheeks and taste the scent of sage. Patrick, he glumly reflected, could do neither.

When they entered, Darby was awed by the size and complexity of the machinery at work.

"Huge, isn't it?" McKenna said.

"I never imagined it would be so big."

"Over there is the blacksmith shop where we have two men who do nothing but sharpen picks and drills," he said, pointing. "And right beside it is our timber shop where the lumber used as supports is framed to be sent below as quick as it's needed. All done by circular saws, powered by steam."

"Astounding."

McKenna nodded. "It's a big operation and we're modernizing to cut costs. Our machine shop is another example. Used to be, we had blacksmiths, now there are skilled ironworkers using a steam engine to run planers, lathes, and such."

"Where's the main shaft?" Darby asked eagerly.

"This way."

Darby followed. He actually knew very little about machinery and really had no interest in it at this moment. He was far too preoccupied with his dark thoughts concerning the boy who worked somewhere deep underground. Yet he half-listened to McKenna and gathered that everything ran by steam. The room was full of it and great warm clouds drifted up to towering ceilings to condense and drip to the floor below. He imagined it to be like walking through a man-made tropical rain forest. The employees he saw moved among the clanking engines, groaning wheels, and pumps as purposefully as their machines. It was kind of eerie, perhaps a glimpse of an approaching industrial age he somehow dreaded.

"There she is," McKenna pointed, "the mine shaft."

Darby hesitated before drawing closer. He glanced at the superintendent and saw him nod reassuringly. Out of the ground, hissing steam rose in a billowing cloud. Then, before his disbelieving eyes, Darby saw a cage emerge from the vapor and jolt to a standstill. Men, bare chested and sweating profusely, disembarked and shuffled wearily away.

The writer swallowed dryly. He hadn't been sure what to expect, but certainly not this. To step into the flimsy cage, engulfed in swirling steam, and then to plunge into the bowels of hell was more than he'd bargained for.

McKenna stepped in close. "First time anyone sees it, they want to back down. If you've a mind, you can wait until I send for him to come up later."

"No," Darby replied, studying the cage. If he were going to write about mining, sooner or later he had to do this. He might as well get it over with. The cage wasn't really a cage at all, but more like a platform about four feet square, without even the protection of siding. It quivered waiting for them to mount and Darby eyed the thin steel braid of cable which lowered the contraption.

"It'll hold, don't worry," McKenna said, jumping onto the platform.

Darby followed, but the cage swayed underfoot while his stomach rolled and his mouth went dry. He wasn't a coward, but suspended above the black, steaming hole, he wished he'd waited to do this some other time.

McKenna nodded to the hoisting engineer and Darby gripped a piece of metalwork and watched the engineer prepare to send them to what he hoped wasn't eternity. Just before the earth dropped out from under his feet, he read the sign posted beside the operator. NO PERSON IS ALLOWED TO SPEAK TO THE ENGINEERS WHILE ON DUTY. DISTRACTIONS CAUSE FATALITIES!

Darby gasped. The steam caused him to feel as if he were standing in water and the impact of the sign made him want to leap from the fragile cage and run. But it was too late. The engineer jammed a lever forward and the big hoisting reel about which the braided cable wound began to spin.

Darby stifled a cry as everything went black and his insides seemed to climb up through his mouth with a sickening, weightless feeling. He strangled the cage with both hands and was determined that, should the flimsy platform drop loose, he was going to survive by hanging on.

Seconds felt like hours as they fell unseeing deeper and deeper. Darby opened his eyes and saw, like the winking of fireflies, blurring lights as they plummeted through one working level toward another. Just a flash of light, a glimpse of half-clothed men, a murmur of shouts, the clash of machinery as they shot through the roof of a cavern and then dropped through its floor.

It was ghastly, yet as the moments passed, Darby felt an exhilaration. The cage would hold and . . . wasn't its rate of descent slackening?

Yes!

Where before there had been weightlessness, Darby now felt the opposite. As the cage braked, he felt his stomach drop through his very knees and his bones seemed to compress downward through his ankles. Then, it was over.

"You can let go now, Mr. Buckingham. We're at the nine hundred-foot level station."

Darby nodded, certain his voice would squeak if he tried to talk. He staggered off the cage.

McKenna reached over and hammered a bell on the side of the cage. "It's the only way the hoisting engineer knows what's going on down here," he explained. "It works just like a telegraph and the engineer knows its sound far better than that of his own voice. Has to."

Darby cleared his throat. "That's why the sign up above?"

"Yep," McKenna said, "if his ear strays more than four inches from the bell, we fire him. Got to be that way or you'll have accidents and, in mining, they're usually fatal. Come on, let's go find young Cassidy."

As they walked across the room, Darby Buckingham heard McKenna explain that the stations were the places of landing at each of the working mine levels. They were generally at hundred-foot intervals and, like this one, they were huge and roomy affairs supported by heavy timbering. At each station, miners and ore were transferred as the men changed shifts.

Darby ran his forefinger across his brow and shook off the sweat. The heat was punishing. "How hot is it?"

"Oh, about a hundred and six. Temperature climbs five degrees every station. When we get to one hundred and twenty degrees, the men start cramping up and getting dizzy. That's when work gets expensive. They just can't do much for long in those conditions. Not even with all the ice we provide them."

"What's going on?" Darby asked, pointing to a cluster of men gathered about a miner tacking up sheets of paper while pulling others down.

"Latest stock market reports. Every time the shift changes or the San Francisco Stock Board makes a sudden move—up or down—we send a runner from the telegraph office and the prices are passed below. Most of these fellas live or die by their stocks. They all own one kind or another."

Darby walked over to the newly posted sheets and heard a few of the men swearing while others crowed happily. They were all discussing Emerald.

"Damn!" someone cussed, "I sold it for only ten bucks a share. Now would you look at it!"

"I did the same. We all did," others grumbled. "Where's that Cassidy boy? The least he coulda done is tipped us off."

"Hell, he don't know nothin'. Told me he doesn't even own any himself."

"Where is he?" Darby asked, breaking through the talk.

Several men turned away from the papers. "He's workin' on down the line. That kid is a mule for work. Hardly ever takes a break, 'cept to relieve himself."

"This way," McKenna motioned and Darby, his face grim and set, followed.

The boy, his face streaked with perspiration, looked so thin and weak that Darby had trouble paying attention to his words.

"The truth is, sir, we once had a lot of that stock.

Then, dammit, after everything went bad, we had to
sell most for whatever we could."

"But did you sell *all* of it?" Darby asked. "Certainly
you must have kept some."

The boy looked away suddenly. "Not to be disre-
spectful, sir, I know you're the one who took a beating
to help, but . . ." His words died.

"Patrick," Darby said quickly, "I've talked to Mr.
McKenna and he tells me you're living down here.
Working extra time. Why?"

The boy squared his shoulders. "If it's all the same
to you, sir, I'd rather not talk about it Now, if you
don't mind, I'd best get back to work."

He turned and started to leave. Darby reached out
and gently gripped the thin shoulder and felt Patrick
stiffen.

"I'll not be laid a hand on, sir!"

Darby nodded. "Just listen to me for a moment
before you go," he said, pulling his hand away.

Beside him, McKenna fidgeted uncomfortably. "I've
got a few things to look after. Patrick, I'm not ordering
you to hear Mr. Buckingham, but I do think you owe
him that much."

The fire in the Irish lad's eyes died and he nodded
his head, but Darby saw that his fists were clenched.
When the superintendent walked away, Darby tried to
think of a way to reach his unwilling listener.

"Patrick," he began, "you must have heard about
your mine. The stock has risen dramatically this very
morning. That means, even if you have only a few
shares, you can afford to quit working day and night in
this hell. It's not good for your health."

Patrick smiled. A thin, very white smile of teeth in
that work-blackened face. It wasn't a happy smile
though, and coming from a thirteen-year-old it seemed
ageless and knowing. "It's not so bad, Mr. Buckingham. The others down here treat me good. And as for
day and night, well, it's all one and the same nine
hundred feet into the rock."

Darby couldn't argue the point, yet he was determined not to give in. "A young man like you requires sunlight and fresh air to grow and become strong."

"It just doesn't matter anymore," Patrick said in a dull voice.

"What do you mean, it doesn't matter! Of course it does. If you're worried about Conrad Trent, don't be. I'll guarantee your safety."

The boy said nothing as they looked into each other's eyes. Darby wanted to reach out and physically carry him over to the cage and out of this place. But he didn't. Something in the set of Patrick Cassidy's expression told him not to.

"Mr. Buckingham, I'm mighty grateful to you for what you did and I'll offer my thanks here and now." He stuck out his hand and, when Darby took it in his own, it felt as rough as a horse's hoof, hard and scaled with ridges of callous across the palm.

"Now, sir, if you're done with me I must go back to work."

"Blast!" Darby exploded, "Why won't you let me help?"

"There's nothing anyone can change now."

Darby tried once more. "Just one last question. How much Emerald stock did your brother keep?"

"Twenty-five percent. An even two hundred and fifty shares."

"Then you're still a wealthy young man with plenty of money to send home," Darby said flatly. "There's nothing to keep you down here any longer!"

Patrick tried to keep a brave face, but couldn't. "The stocks are gone," he said brokenly. "They were taken off Quinn's body."

"What!" Darby rocked back.

The boy nodded, pretended something was making his eyes water. "I snuck back to the mortuary and . . . and said goodbye to Quinn. When I reached inside his coat pocket where he always carried the stock certificates, they weren't there."

"What then?"

"I waited all night and, when the undertaker came

in, I demanded what was rightly mine. He started yelling. Told me to get out or he'd send for one of Mr. Trent's men."

"Blast! I'll wring his neck."

"No use, Mr. Buckingham. Those stocks are gone. My bet is that Mr. Trent took 'em."

While Darby silently raged at the injustice of the world, Patrick Cassidy walked away. And there wasn't a damn thing, in that moment, that Darby could do or say to stop him.

"I'll be back," he yelled so loudly men turned to watch. "You take care of yourself. Put on some weight and you'll be stronger. I'll see you and when I do, I'll have your stock, even if I have to wring Conrad Trent's neck. I swear I will!"

Patrick Cassidy didn't call back or even turn around. He just kept shuffling down the drift tunnel. A thin, weary little figure who'd probably heard too many promises to care anymore. He'd stated his feelings clearly.

It just didn't matter anymore.

That's when Darby realized what the boy meant. He was going to work as long as his body would move and every penny he earned would go to pay off a family debt. And, when he couldn't go on, well, the debt would be paid. Patrick never planned to see the light of day again.

This understanding made Darby Buckingham hurry toward the cage, shouting for McKenna. Some way or other, he *had* to get the stock back or the young man was going to work himself to death.

Patrick was too proud to take charity but not what was rightfully his. It was the Emerald certificates or nothing. There was no other way. It all started with Conrad Trent.

Dolly Beavers felt she was ready to make an investment in the Comstock mines. For days, while Zack and Bear had rumbled about, sampling the whiskey in every saloon in town, Dolly found out all she could about the geology of Sun Mountain. She was convinced that a proper understanding of the Comstock Lode was essential to a wise investment.

With her charm and good looks, there was no trouble getting men to expound on all sorts of theories about how the Comstock had been formed. The problem lay in weeding out misconception from truth. Fortunately, she'd been able to obtain the advice of an educated geologist named Mr. Leroy Thomas. He'd been referred to her by that nice young bank teller.

After hearing so many conflicting stories, it was refreshing to find an expert who could give her a reasoned and instructive account of the matter.

According to Mr. Thomas, the Virginia range of mountains was separated from the Sierra Nevadas by a giant volcanic upheaval. That was why, on their eastern side where the lode ran, the rock was volcanic in origin and called propylite. As the great masses shifted during those early days, a fissure occurred, nearly four miles in length and up to two thousand feet deep. The rendering apart of rock created great heat, and into the fissure burst immense quantities of water which quickly began to boil from the molten hells below earth, flushing upward great quantities of ores rich in gold and silver.

Ages passed. The trapped elements seethed like a cauldron and bubbled until huge bodies of quartz formed on its steaming walls and the mineral impurities were melted away, leaving only the purer elements of gold and silver in the quartz. Each type of precious metal was so rich and pure from the heat that you could scrape it away from the encapsulating quartz with your fingernail.

Dolly had listened almost transfixed with the images Mr. Thomas laid out with his shaping hands. But then a question had jumped into her nimble mind. If the ore body was like a great convoluted silk stocking filled with riches, why then might one mine shaft puncture the stocking and another only twenty feet away miss it entirely?

Mr. Thomas had shown a flicker of irritation and seemed to think about it for a few moments before answering. Finally, he admitted that hers was a difficult question and that his theory was that the tremendous weight of the volcanic rock had finally begun to collapse as the gases and waters ate at it from below. Thus were created the ravines and irregular surfaces of the Comstock. As the Virginia mountain range settled and slumped into the soupy masses below, parts of the stocking were flattened while others squeezed out in a balloon fashion. In short, the form became irregular and distorted by nature until it bore no resemblance at all to its original shape. Some of the boiling substances had even managed to escape through the hot mineral pools which could be seen around the countryside all the way to Reno.

Despite this problem, he assured her, to know the size and general direction of the lode was to know its greatest secret. And then, Mr. Thomas would say no more.

After she'd left, Dolly talked it over with Bear and Zack though they'd acted bored. But all had agreed Thomas knew his stuff and she should make him get down to specifics. So today she was on her way back to the geologist's office, prepared to hire the man's services. Dolly, not to leave anything to chance, had dressed in her finest and fixed her long blond tresses in their most becoming arrangement. She was as irresistible as she could make herself.

When she reached the office, Dolly inspected herself in the window and then entered with a stunning smile on her face. She crossed a small waiting room and headed toward his office, reminding herself to inquire about that Emerald stock everyone was raving about.

Just as she was about to knock and enter, a loud shout caused her to recoil.

"Mr. Thomas! In the name of decency, I demand you return that widow's funds and cease this sham business!"

Dolly's eyes widened. She took a sideways step and peeked through the crack in the open doorway before ducking back out of sight. Though she'd caught only a glimpse of the scene in the geologist's office, it had been enough. Mr. Leroy Thomas was seated at his desk while another man waited with stiff impatience.

"Sham business!" Thomas cried. "I'll have you know, Mr. Conrad Trent, that I am a licensed geologist with the American . . ."

"Hogwash, man! I've just finished an investigation of your so-called credentials at my own expense. You're a fraud!"

Dolly gasped and leaned forward intently as Trent's bitter accusations continued. "You are no more licensed than I am. You never went to school and all those high-sounding theories you exhort are nothing but cleverly concocted lies designed to dupe the innocent."

Dolly's heart was pounding. She could almost hear it beat in the silence that crowded the office. Could this be true!

Then Leroy Thomas, his voice as cold as spring run-off, laughed. It was so ominous and hate-filled that Dolly shivered when the laughter ended and the man spoke. "Mr. Trent, my congratulations on your investigation. I confess to my deception."

"You admit it openly?"

"Of course not! What I've said is between us and I'm offering my services to you, fully aware that you cannot fail to see how profitable we could be for one another."

Dolly heard the stockbroker reply, "How so?"

"Oh, come now. You're the most respected speculator on this mountain. And as far as the rest of Virginia City is concerned, I'm the only legitimate geologist on the Comstock. Between us, we could make a fortune. Think of it, Mr. Trent! Why, right now, I have a lady with two partners worth thirty thousand dollars just itching to invest in any worthless piece of property I say. I'm scouting for a piece of rock I can buy for almost nothing and sell to her. If you wish, I'll cut you in on the profits. It's foolproof, I tell you. Thirty thousand dollars, just like that." Dolly heard his fingers snap. "I'm waiting for your answer, Mr. Trent."

The geologist didn't have to wait long. Dolly Beavers, her lips pressed together in cold fury, heard a sharp, cracking sound of flesh on bone and then a loud crash.

"There's my answer to corruption!"

"Good for you!" Dolly shouted, leaping into the doorway.

Both men, one a thief with a bleeding lip and his backside on the floor, and the other a magnificent gentleman with raised fists, turned their attentions to Dolly.

"Miss Beavers," Thomas cried, struggling to get to his feet, "I didn't . . ."

"Of course you didn't, you scoundrel!" Dolly strode over to the man and slapped his face so hard he staggered. "I heard everything!"

She turned away from him with disgust and, when she gazed into Conrad Trent's eyes, she couldn't help but think he was one of the most wonderful, handsome, and honorable men she'd ever met.

"Mr. Trent, my name is *Miss* Dolly Beavers." Her eyelashes fluttered expertly. "And it seems I owe my total good fortune to you at this moment."

"Madam," he said, smiling widely and bowing at the waist, "it is every man who owes *you* a debt, merely for being allowed to witness your loveliness."

Dolly's heart leapt in her breast. "Why," she gushed, "that's the most beautiful compliment I've ever received!"

"If you say so," he said agreeably. "Now, if I may be so bold as to ask you to accompany me from this . . . this viper's den, would you join me for lunch?"

Would she! Dolly made herself count to five before answering. It never paid to sound too eager. "Yes, I believe I will!"

As they started to leave, Mr. Trent advised the fraudulent and thoroughly castigated Leroy Thomas to take down his phony license and college diploma at once.

"But what about the money?" Dolly asked, as they strolled down the boardwalk.

"Money? What money?"

"You know, that poor widow's funds?"

"Oh, yes!" Conrad Trent shook his head angrily. "I *knew* there was something I'd forgotten. But . . ."

She stopped him. Looked into his eyes. "But, what . . . Mr. Trent?"

"Well," he laughed, almost boyishly, "when I saw your face, I . . . I just forgot everything else."

Shivering corsets! This man was something!

She looked away, feeling her cheeks warm pleasantly. "Shall we go back?"

"Oh, no! I'll go later. Perhaps after we've eaten."

"Are you sure it's safe?" Dolly asked, concern edging her voice.

Conrad Trent chuckled out loud as she took his strong arm. "Yes, my dear, I'm sure. Very."

FIVE

Conrad Trent did not return to collect the fictitious widow's money after lunch. Instead . . . he rented a carriage and took Miss Dolly Beavers for a ride across the Comstock. Everywhere they traveled that afternoon, Conrad saw the looks of envy cast by the rough miners. More than one said outright that she was the most beautiful woman he'd ever seen.

That kind of attention, he felt, greatly enhanced his own standing and he couldn't help but compare himself to a king surveying his domain. What made him feel especially proud was that Miss Beavers completely ignored the responses she seemed to generate and made him feel that he was the only man in the world.

At sundown, Conrad topped Gold Hill Canyon and pulled the carriage off the road right at the crest of the Divide which separated the Silver City and Gold Hill communities from Virginia City. To the east, they could see a vast panorama of gray and purple mountains that stretched beyond the range of the human eye. Harsh, brutal country, where few men ventured. Yet now, in the fading light, it all appeared somehow more gentle and at peace.

They sat in close stillness as the day ended and saw a thousand and more campfires spring to life on both sides of the Divide. Conrad knew that later he would write a poem about this moment and compare it to witnessing the birth of some vast night army. Farther to the south, the last snows glowed like silver crowns on the tallest kings of the marching Sierra Nevadas.

Beside him, Dolly sat quietly, her eyes filled with the incredible beauty of it all. Conrad struggled for words to express how he felt at that moment—about the Comstock and the woman.

> "In shadows soft with muted gold
> I gaze upon this land, seeing
> its beauty unfold.
> Why, I wonder, did I never see
> this all before?
> It must be, dear Dolly, that
> your beauty opened my eyes
> forevermore."

He saw her lips tremble, the perfect silhouette of her mouth change as she whispered, "That's the most beautiful, poetic thing ever said to me, Mr. Trent."

For once in his life, Conrad failed to come up with a response. All through the day, he'd been aware that this woman was getting a grip on him even though his intentions were strictly criminal. He would cheat her out of her money because that was his nature. But . . . but she was going to make him feel terrible doing it.

"Conrad, it's almost dark," she said, "though I hate to see this day end."

"It needn't," he replied quickly. "Come to dinner with me. Afterward, we'll go to a small tavern where only a select membership is allowed."

Dolly's laughter tinkled over the Divide. "Really, Conrad, I think . . ."

She never quite finished. He hadn't meant to kiss her, not yet, but he did. Her lips were incredibly soft and, though she resisted somewhat, the very act of her doing so made her even more desirable.

"Mr. Trent!" she cried, trying to sound offended but, he was sure, feeling quite the opposite. "If we're to see each other again, I insist you learn to control yourself."

Conrad felt good. Very good. "That's going to be quite difficult, Miss Beavers. Yet I promise to at least make the attempt."

She looked down at her hands a moment and he saw her expression grow sad.

"Is there anything else wrong?" he asked, suddenly anxious. "Was my kiss so distasteful?"

"No," she replied, after a period so long he'd seen two stars blink into existence. "It's just that . . . well, it's just that I'm in love with Mr. Darby Buckingham."

If she'd struck him between the eyes with an axe handle, the effect couldn't have been more stunning. His first impulse was to take her back into his arms and show her how a real man could make a woman feel. Yet, he did nothing because he knew that whatever he said or did would reflect his bitterness and, therefore, be unfavorably received.

"Git up, horse!" he snapped, cracking it hard on the backside.

He drove in silence for several minutes until he was certain he could hide the anger in his voice. And when he finally spoke, it was in almost a conversational tone.

"Miss Beavers, what you've told me about your feelings concerning Mr. Buckingham does not change my intentions of escorting you to dinner and a full evening of entertainment. Are you . . . betrothed?"

"No," she said shortly.

"Good! As for your declaration of love, I shall test it. *What the eye doth once behold, can sometimes grow mighty old.*"

"Meaning?"

"Meaning, for example, until this evening, I always thought those eastern mountains were pretty ugly. With you, I saw them in a whole different light. Perhaps you will find it revealing to watch, in the days to come, how your Mr. Buckingham stacks up against me."

He waited for her answer and, when it didn't come, he swallowed his pride. "Give me a chance, Miss Beavers. That's all I'm asking."

"All right," she said quickly. "That's reasonable. But I must confess I had another reason for accepting your invitation today."

"What other reason?"

"I want you to help me and my friends to invest our money in stocks. I've . . . I've been hearing a great deal of excitement over the Emerald claim. Do you think it a good investment?"

Twenty-four hours earlier, Conrad Trent would have laughed outright at how easily it came. He hadn't even needed to bring up the subject; here it was—Miss Beavers was laying the thirty thousand at his feet.

"Mr. Trent," she was saying, "I feel almost ashamed that I might have misled you. If those were my initial motives, they've changed."

"Have they?"

"Oh yes, though I am still in great need of your excellent advice. It's very important that I not lose, because two-thirds of what I have to invest isn't even mine. Please, help me."

He should have been laughing inside—but he wasn't. "Miss Beavers, don't worry about a thing. Emerald stock is solid and I'll purchase some for you first thing in the morning. You and your partners will be making a sound investment."

"Oh thank you, Conrad!" She leaned over and gave him an astonishingly powerful hug. Then, she planted a smacking kiss on his cheek.

"I'm so happy you're not angry."

He swallowed a bad taste in his mouth. "I feel just fine, my dear," he mumbled. That was a lie. Conrad Trent felt awful. He would have given anything if the thirty thousand dollars had belonged to Darby Buckingham or someone else. But it didn't and there was no way he could change what had to be.

Conrad hoped Dolly wasn't offended by drink. It was going to take quite a few to make him feel better. Maybe an entire bottle. My God, he thought bleakly, why couldn't the woman have been ugly, or pretentious, or grasping, or manipulative?

Sadly, Dolly Beavers was none of those things. Only lovely, spontaneous, the possessor of thirty thousand dollars, and one hell of a fine appreciation for his own brilliant poetry.

Darby Buckingham tracked them down although the hour was very late. He felt weary from too much tromping around. His shoes were scratched from the brush and his clothes dusty from the constant wind-blown dirt which seemed a part of the Comstock. But even though he was not presentable, he marched up to the door of the private Silver Crystal Club and knocked loudly.

A powerful man opened it and inspected Darby critically. "Members only," he said with clear satisfaction.

"I'm looking for Conrad Trent and Miss Dolly Beavers. I'm told they came here tonight."

"Mr. Trent didn't tell me to expect anyone else. Shove off, buster."

As the door was closing, Darby reached for it with his left hand. But he wasn't quite fast enough and the burly doorman slammed it, crushing the knuckles of his fingers.

"Blast!" Darby roared, pain shooting clear up his arm. With savage fury, he grabbed the door handle with his free hand and, with a tremendous heave, he tore it open.

"Damn you! I said . . ."

Darby glanced at his fingers. They were numb and blood oozed from under the nails.

"They're broken," he hissed. With that pronouncement, his anger exploded and he grabbed the doorman with his right hand, balled up his coat front, and flung him against the building.

The man cried out, tried to throw a punch, but Darby never let him regain his balance. Though his left hand was out of commission, his right was all he needed. Three times more, he pounded the big doorman into the wall until the man's head rolled sideways and his eyes lost focus.

Darby hurled him into the street and charged inside. The interior was large, at least fifty feet square, and elegant by anyone's standards. Near the front of the room, patrons who'd no doubt felt the nearby wall shake were wide-eyed as he came through. His derby was knocked askew and his eyes, black and smoldering, swept over the tables like a withering flame.

Then, his head snapped around and he studied the far end of the room. There was a sizable crowd and many hadn't yet realized a wild man had entered their flock. Darby saw couples dancing to piano music. And square on the center of the floor, he saw Conrad Trent waltzing Dolly Beavers.

Darby failed to appreciate what a beautiful couple they made and how gracefully they danced together. He was anything but graceful as he bulled through the crowd. Several men complained loudly but he didn't care. If they were still of a mind for trouble, he'd accommodate them on the exit. Right now, he wanted Conrad Trent.

He was almost upon them when Dolly saw him and yelled, "Darby!"

His warning gave Trent just enough time to pivot and then Darby one-handed him by the collar and threw him into the piano player.

"Darby no, please!"

While the two men untangled themselves on the floor, Dolly grabbed the stockbroker and dragged him erect.

"I'm here for that two hundred and fifty shares of Emerald stock you took off the body of Quinn Cassidy. I want it now!"

"Go to hell, Buckingham!" he spat, breaking free and stepping away.

Darby went after him. Forgetting about his injury, he pumped a left hook into Trent's belly. The man gasped, but his pain was as nothing compared to Darby's. Those broken fingers sent enough agony up through his shoulder to paralyze him for an instant. Conrad Trent proved he hadn't lied about one thing— the man could fight.

While Darby swayed with pain, Trent recovered fast enough to land two hard blows to the writer's jaw. Darby rocked back and was about to come at him one-handed when Trent pulled a derringer out of his coat sleeve.

"One more step and you're dead!"

"No!" Dolly cried, throwing herself between them. "Please don't shoot him!"

Darby hesitated, unwilling to take the risk that Trent might fire. Besides, there was no point in foolishly charging in to his death. He swayed with indecision. How could he make Dolly and these people see the truth? They were Trent's friends, but maybe he could expose the stockbroker for the cheat that he most surely was. It was worth a try.

"I just came back from seeing Patrick Cassidy," he began. "You've all heard the story. What hasn't been told is that his dead brother had, in his possession, two hundred and fifty shares. They were stolen after Trent killed him."

"In self defense!" Trent yelled. "Everyone knows that."

"Do they know you own almost all of the Emerald stock?" Darby challenged. "And that you purposefully led the Cassidys into issuing so much that the value had to drop to nothing?"

Trent leered. "If that were true, why did I then, as you accuse, buy up those stocks?"

Darby felt the sweat pop up on his body. "Because the Emerald *is* worth a fortune."

He hadn't meant to say that and wasn't even sure that it was true. Damn his inferior knowledge of mining stock! Trent had the advantage.

He used it.

"If . . . let's just suppose, the Emerald actually is worth a fortune as you've stated. Then, if I really did own so much of its stock, why . . . would . . . I . . . sell?"

Darby shuddered. He couldn't answer. He was beaten.

A number of the men crowded around the dance floor began to snort and jeer at him. That didn't hurt nearly as much as the look he saw on Dolly Beaver's lovely face. It wasn't contempt. No, she was far too much woman for that. It was . . . pity. Pity for a man she loved and had respected, but might never again.

Darby swallowed his defeat. Never in his life had he been so humiliated and felt so helpless. Helpless because he knew he was right and yet, yet he didn't understand how to unravel the deception behind Trent's plan.

"We're all waiting for your answer," Trent said, grinning broadly and winking at several of his friends. "I'm as curious as anyone why I would sell a mine for a fraction of its real value."

Dolly, bless her heart, came to his side. "I'm ready to leave," she told him in a cracked voice. "You don't have to answer that question tonight."

At that moment, he loved her more than anything in the world and he would have exited except for the triumphant leer on Trent's handsome face. Because of it, he just couldn't go.

"I still want that stock for Patrick," he said doggedly, "one way or the other."

Trent's expression changed. He studied Darby for a long moment and his eyes dropped down to the bloody fingers, the hand that was already swollen half again its size. He grinned suddenly. "All right, you can *earn* that stock. At its current value, it's worth over fifteen thousand dollars. I'll put it up if you match it."

"Match it?"

"Yes. I'll have a boxing ring set up right in the middle of C Street. Winner take all and we fight by the new Queensbury Rules like gentlemen. We'll wear gloves, and there will be no wrestling, gouging, or kicking. No striking of a man who's down on one knee and three minute rounds with one minute rest in between."

"I'd rather fight by the London Prize Ring Rules. Bare knuckles, a round ends when one of us falls. No ring. We scratch the line and toe up on either side like men."

"No," Trent said flatly. "My way or none. And to sweeten the pot a little, we'll set up stands and charge admission. The proceeds can go to a charity of the winner's selection."

There was a hum of approval. Several people clapped enthusiastically.

Darby tried to move his fingers and couldn't. He wanted bare knuckles because he'd have a better chance of knocking Trent out with one punch.

"Why the silence, Mr. Buckingham?" He looked about the crowd. "This . . . this caricature of a boor was once a champion. Those who follow the sport have heard of his fame. But now . . . now, we know why he quit. Lack of guts."

"I'll meet you," Darby graveled, his voice shaking with passion. "State the time and place."

"The ring can be constructed tomorrow. The next day is Sunday. We want a good crowd for charity. Sunday is best."

"Sunday it is, then!"

While the crowd hummed with anticipation, Dolly's voice rose over them all. "This is wrong. Please, I don't want to see either of you hurt."

"I'll be fine," Trent offered. "We've had a lovely evening. Will you celebrate with me Sunday night?"

"Oh, men!" Dolly shrieked. Then, she grabbed Darby by the arm and led him through the crowd. Outside, where the air was crisp and still, he realized she was crying.

Because he didn't want to upset her even more by the sight of his crushed and bleeding fingers, Darby shoved them deep into his pocket and tried to find words to make her feel better. He would have liked to take her in his arms but, with one out of action, that would have been noticeably awkward. So he merely patted her on the shoulder.

"There's nothing to cry about, Dolly," he offered.

"Yes, there is," she sniffled, "you . . . you almost got yourself killed in there and you ruined the whole evening for everyone."

Darby recoiled. "Ruined the evening! My God, lady, didn't you hear what I said? Conrad Trent killed a man and swindled a mining claim!"

"No, he didn't," she said angrily. "He told me all

about what happened and everyone knows it was self defense."

Darby's moustache bristled. "If you believe that, I'm afraid I've overestimated your judgment."

"And perhaps I've overestimated yours, Mr. Buckingham! You're the only one in Virginia City who says Mr. Trent didn't merely try to defend himself. And . . ." Her words trailed away.

"Go on, finish what you were going to say. I want to hear the rest."

"Very well." Dolly wiped the tears from her eyes. "Without any evidence at all, you've attacked and slandered a fine man. One I met this very morning in the process of exposing a fraud and returning some dear widow's savings."

"That's preposterous!"

"And, furthermore, it was clear enough out there on the dance floor that you made a fool of yourself with your unfounded and wild claims."

He couldn't believe his ears! It was true he'd acted rashly and couldn't respond to Trent's questions. But that didn't change anything. It meant only that there was more to Trent's devious plan than he'd thought. What *really* bothered him now was Dolly's lack of faith.

"Dolly," he asked, "after what I said, how can you trust him?"

She produced a hanky and blew her nose lustily. "If you'd have seen him this morning in that phony geologist's office and gotten to know him like I did this afternoon . . ."

"What geologist's office?"

"Mr. Leroy Thomas. And, you might not know this, but he writes beautiful poetry."

Darby threw his head back and brayed at the stars.

"Go on and laugh! You never wrote me any poetry, good or bad. And you know what?"

"What?" he said, hearing his laughter echo off the hillsides.

"I think that the reason you dislike him so much is that you're jealous."

"That does it!" he bellowed. "I refuse to listen to another word. I'm taking you back to your hotel room this very moment."

She brushed back a tangle of golden hair that had escaped to fall over her blue eyes. Then she faced him squarely. "I'll go if you admit that you've acted wrongly about Mr. Trent and that you *are* jealous."

"Never!"

Her face seemed to crumple with disappointment, but she recovered enough to say, "Very well, Mr. Buckingham, then I'll return inside. Mr. Trent will be happy to escort me."

"Dolly!"

"It's no use. And, furthermore, I think it's terrible, as strong and experienced with fisticuffs as you are, to take advantage of poor Mr. Trent."

"He made the offer!"

"But you accepted knowing the man doesn't stand a chance. Don't you see!" she pleaded, "he *knows* he'll be beaten and that's his honorable way of giving this Patrick Cassidy boy a free pile of valuable stock."

Darby wanted to tell her about his crushed fingers and how Trent had seen them before making the offer. He also would have liked to tell the woman that Conrad Trent was an experienced boxer himself and undeniably faster—with two hands—than he was going to be with one. But what was the use?

"Dolly, I'm sorry we're parting under these circumstances and, before long, I'll find a way to show you Trent's real character. Until then, I'm going to ask you one favor."

"What is it?" she breathed.

"Don't invest your money, or Zack and Bear's, in Emerald stock. I can't explain how he's going to cheat you. I know only that he will."

Her eyebrows shot up. "You're saying that all he sees in me is my money. It isn't so! You may be a writer, but you haven't the least idea how other men think about me. I've met too many to be fooled by anyone. Not Conrad Trent and not Darby Buckingham. That's why I know you are doing this out of spite and jealousy."

"Spite, no," he said, tight-lipped. "Jealousy? Probably yes." And with that, he turned on his heel and slowly walked away. The emotional ache inside completely obliterated the physical one emanating with steady pulsebeats from his fingers.

Dolly *was* right about the jealousy, but on everything else she was dead wrong. Especially about the fight. Unless a miracle occurred, fighting one-handed he might just get his brains scrambled. That would at least prove to Dolly she'd been incorrect on one account.

The next morning, Darby Buckingham was up and about much earlier than usual. His first order of business was to visit the doctor's office, only to learn what he already knew. The two middle fingers were broken and their book-end partners severely lacerated. Darby had the doctor tape them heavily together in a closed fist. The physician didn't approve, especially when he learned about the upcoming fight. He gravely warned that a single blow could shatter the bone edges.

Darby nodded and left. Several doors farther along the street, he entered a mercantile and bought two pairs of gloves—one extra large and the other his normal size. Then he surprised the storekeeper by leaving one of each pair on the counter.

He ate breakfast across from the hotel and left it half-finished when he saw Zack Woolsey and Bear Timberly emerge for the day.

"Bear, Zack!" he shouted, angling across the street toward them.

They exchanged glances and Darby had the feeling they wanted nothing to do with him.

"Listen," he said, "I know you're angry with me and I admit I behaved poorly when you came into town."

"Poorly is charitable," Zack commented. "What do you want from us?"

"Nothing. All I'm trying to do is to save you from investing your money with Conrad Trent."

Bear hooted. "That's a fine one! We came needing *your* help."

"I'm giving it to you, dammit! Trent is crooked and he's blinded Dolly. If you let her go on listening to him, you'll all go broke."

"Says you. If you'd advised us to buy Emerald stock on the day we came, we'd be rich. Back there in the hotel lobby, the man told me it's gone up to over a hundred dollars a share. Dolly said she'll decide after the fight tomorrow. But, come Monday morning, I reckon we'll buy."

They started to walk on, then Zack twisted around.

"You've changed since coming here, Buckingham. Used to be, you were a right decent fella. Not anymore. All last night, we heard Miss Dolly crying. This morning, we learned it was because of you."

"Yes, but . . ."

"Stay shut of her, Buckingham! We're going to be at that fight tomorrow and hopin' Mr. Trent whips you. Seems you've gotten too gawddammed uppity for your own good. A sound whalloping could be the best medicine. And I hope you get it!"

Darby clamped his mouth shut. To reply would only drive the wedge deeper. Besides, he knew how they felt about Dolly and, if they were convinced he'd caused her pain, then they'd not listen to a word he said.

Darby turned and trudged off, feeling lower in spirit than he could ever remember. So far, he'd lost his friends and his woman. A block away he saw carpenters hauling lumber onto C Street. They were already starting to construct the ring.

"Blast!" he swore. The only good thing that might come out of this whole miserable affair was the charity fund and, if he lost, even the charity money would probably wind up in Trent's pockets. If he won, no good would come of it for himself. Sure, young Patrick Cassidy would get his stock back, yet the price would be dear. Victory would convince Dolly that Trent was some kind of a martyr. It would make her invest the whole thirty thousand in Emerald and drive her into Trent's arms out of misguided sympathy. Any way

Darby turned it around in his mind, it was a no-win proposition.

Only fierce pride and his personal commitment to justice kept the dime novelist from packing his bags and leaving the Comstock.

A thin, wintry smile crossed Darby's lips. He'd never run from a fight. Besides, even that way, Conrad Trent would come out ahead. There was just no solution. Without supporters, it was going to make facing up to the contest that much tougher.

"So be it!" he yelled at the startled carpenters. "So be it!"

SIX

Darby Buckingham stepped out of the mine cage at the nine-hundred foot level of the Consolidated. He was in a hurry and wasted no time in asking a workman for directions. He strode purposefully down the tunnel. On his way, he passed a group of carpenters who were laboriously manhandling a huge timber into its square set position. Farther along, he had to ease around others who were laying track in the tunnel for ore carts.

He rounded a corner and, peering down a corridor of blasted rock, he found Patrick Cassidy. The boy was holding a long steel chisel to the wall while his partner struck it with an eight-pound sledge. As he approached the pair, Darby was impressed by the teamwork involved in double-jack drilling. The blows came little more than a second apart and, after each one, Patrick would turn the chisel to keep it from sticking or binding in the rock. After each ringing crack of steel on steel, a fine rock powder drifted down to the tunnel floor. They were setting holes for blasting.

Neither man noticed him until he was almost upon them. "Why don't you take a rest?" Darby suggested to the muscled hammer wielder. "Mr. McKenna said I could interrupt work for a few minutes."

The man nodded, dropped his sledge and walked away without comment. Patrick slumped to the floor and produced a soiled handkerchief to mop his face.

Once again, Darby was alarmed by the awful weariness in the boy. His skin seemed abnormally pale, so white it looked unnatural in the carbite light being used.

The writer sat beside him. "How are you feeling?"

Patrick stared at his boots. "Fine, sir."

"Good. I need to ask you a question and it won't take long."

"Ask then."

"All right." The boy didn't seem particularly curious about his visit nor encouraged by his interest. Maybe he was just too tired to care about anything. "How valuable is the Emerald Mine?"

"It's a rich strike for sure, Mr. Buckingham. No one knows how rich, because we never got to the hundred-foot level. The ore just kept getting better the further down we mined."

"And that's why you issued stock? So you could buy heavy equipment?"

"Yes. But when the stock fell, we ran out of money before we hit the high-paying dirt. Our new steam engine was still in a crate when the money man came and took it away. You can't mine deeper than sixty feet without machinery."

Darby scowled as he pictured how it must have been. The Cassidys had issued more and more stock, trying to accumulate enough capital to mechanize. They'd come up short and, in the process, lost everything.

"How much farther would you have had to go before you struck high grade ore?"

"We talked about that plenty, me and Quinn. Both of us figured maybe thirty feet. My brother said once we got that far, nothing would stand in our way."

"But you ran out of time and money. That's why the Emerald is all boarded up and a guard is posted."

"Yeah. Probably on Trent's payroll." He paused. "Why are you asking me these questions?"

"Because, if Trent now owns your stock, and the Emerald is rich, I must find out why he's selling."

"I can't answer that," Patrick admitted. "Seems like

he'd have the money to mine it himself and make a fortune. Mr. Buckingham?"

"Yes?"

Patrick looked down at the floor, absently kicked a piece of gravel. "I heard about what you tried to do at the Crystal Club and about the fight."

Darby pushed his left hand deeper into his pocket. Patrick already had enough to worry about.

"I also heard the bet."

"News travels fast," Darby commented.

"Sure does. Half the men on this level have already asked the boss for a few hours off to see the fight. There will be a lot of money riding on it."

Darby shrugged. There always had been when he'd fought. Why should it be any different now? "Are you betting?"

"I'm not sure. You . . ." he stumbled for words, "you shouldn't fight Trent."

"Do you think he'll whip me?"

"I don't know," Patrick said honestly. "But all the spectators will be on his side and Trent is bound to load things in his favor. You can be sure the referee will be on his payroll."

"I wish we were fighting according to Jack Boughton's London Prize Ring Rules," Darby said angrily. "That's the way it ought to be done. A twenty-four foot ring and a line drawn across the center for a pair of good men to toe the mark." He shook his head, remembering battles of yesterday. "When I fought, a round wasn't over until a man fell. He had thirty seconds before the referee called 'Time' and, if he wasn't up to the scratch mark, he was counted out."

Darby thought back on his prize fighting days with some wistfulness. It hadn't been a respectable calling then, not really. He well-remembered how the sport had been outlawed in nearly every state with some even calling for prison terms for violators. But he never had been caught. The word of a fight would go out, but its exact time and location were always a last minute secret. He recalled a cold day in February of 1849 when he'd fought John Byers. They'd had to set sail from Baltimore to find a place where the fight could be staged without police interference.

What a merry chase that had been, with a vessel full of militia bent on stopping the fight in hot pursuit! The overhead sails had been taut with a good wind, and they'd finally outstripped their pursuers. With more than three hundred fight fans, they'd beached on a lonely section of the Maryland coast.

While Darby and John Byers stripped down to their tight pants and boots spiked for purchase and, sometimes, even trampling, the eager spectators had constructed a proper ring using stakes cut from the forest. Ring ropes were hauled down from the boat's rigging and the thin cover of snow was brushed from the chosen turf. They'd boot-stomped the ring until it was flat and hard-packed.

Byers had towered over him, but their weights were nearly identical. In the first round, Byers had connected with a straight blow to the nose and been cheered for taking first blood. Odds changed accordingly and everyone drank faster.

By the third round, Darby had closed his opponent's right eye but damaged a knuckle in the process. By the seventh round, John Byers' ribs were purple and his gasps for air blew thick vapor clouds into Darby's face.

The ground was frozen and they slipped often, so the rounds weren't long. In the nineteenth, Byers got his arm around Darby's neck and tried to choke him on the ropes, a desperate but legal maneuver. Darby had somehow managed to trip Byers and they'd both spilled out of the ring, thus ending another round. When they came to scratch in the twentieth, Darby had belted the man with a right uppercut just below the breast-bone. Byer's swollen and distended face had drained of blood and Darby, knowing his own strength was fading, had unloaded a flurry of vicious punches that were calculated to keep Byers on his feet until he'd gone down to stay.

Darby's winner-take-all purse had earned him six hundred dollars. But, as was his custom, he'd stood before the crowd and demanded they pass the hat around for the vanquished. He'd heard later that John Byers had gotten thirty-four dollars plus change and was grateful to have it. A good man, that John, they'd become good friends while sharing whiskey on the return trip to Baltimore.

"Mr. Buckingham?"

Darby shook out of his daydream and grinned a little sheepishly for allowing his mind to wander so far.

"Yes?"

"I'm going to be up there in your corner."

Darby was touched. He knew the boy's offer carried risk, yet there was no one else he could expect to attend to his ministrations between rounds. "I can't guarantee your safety. I'll have my hands full of my own work."

Patrick nodded. "I don't mean to sound ungrateful, but I know Conrad Trent. He can't lose."

Darby sniffed with contempt. "He's not half the man John Byers was."

"Who?"

"Never mind," Darby said. "I'll see you tomorrow."

That night, Darby stayed in his room. Out in the street, he could hear people talking about Sunday's big event. The money was going three to one with Conrad Trent as the favorite. Just before he drifted off to sleep, Darby wondered if Dolly Beavers thought that he'd lose. Probably not. But then she didn't know about his broken fingers.

If they had been fighting by the old London Prize Ring Rules, he would be much more confident because he knew all the tricks and ploys it took to win besides a good punch and a hard jaw. But with gloves and rest periods, it was going to be difficult to beat Trent. Undoubtedly, the man was in better shape, though not nearly as strong. Unless he missed his guess, Darby thought Trent would be doing a lot of dancing and jabbing. He'd avoid close punching because of his inferior arm power.

Darby flexed his huge biceps and they were as hard and reassuring as ever. He fell asleep dreaming of how he'd corner Trent and knock him flat with a single blow—the way he'd done so many times before.

The size and frenzy of the crowd was beyond all expectations as Darby approached the ring. When they saw him, stripped to the waist in his fighting togs, a hush fell over them and a few men jumped out of the stands to change their bets. He was massive in the upper body, so powerfully built in the arms and shoulders that no one noticed the few extra pounds he now carried about the waist.

He didn't look at any of them as he continued forward and men parted to let him pass. Darby's face was freshly shaven and his moustache carefully trimmed. Atop his head, he wore the characteristic derby hat which had become his trademark in those days. He showed no emotion. Neither fear nor confidence. He looked like a moving slab of granite.

Out of the corner of his eye, he saw the ring officials; one held a bell to signal the rounds and another had a stopwatch. The writer hid his disappointment when he reached his corner and Dolly, Bear, and Zack weren't there to support him.

A woman called his name and Darby spun around. "Dolly . . ." He cut off his words and made himself smile. "Miss Bulette."

"She's going to help me out," said Patrick Cassidy, edging in around her.

"That's very generous. I'll do my best to see your task doesn't amount to much of anything."

Before she could answer, a roar sounded from the onlookers and Darby watched Conrad Trent, surrounded by admirers and dressed in a flowing purple robe, advance toward the ring. When he met the ropes, he upraised his arms for silence. Then, with a flourish, he swept off his hat and tossed it into the square, yelling, "My hat is in the ring!"

Darby Buckingham listened to the thundering ovation which accompanied Conrad Trent's arrival and it made his moustache bristle. The man was a cheap theatrical talent and those fools could shout their lungs raw while he postured about on center stage. Let him take his bows while he could, because Darby figured to bring the curtain down fast. Still, as he watched even the ring officials applaud, he felt a stirring of apprehension. In case of the slightest foul, these judges would disqualify him.

To hell with it! Darby threw his own derby inside and, to his horror and disgust, Trent walked over and stomped it flat.

Instantly, Darby was through the ropes and going for the man. A body of Trent's handlers stepped in between and blocked his path. In the crush of bodies and confusion, someone struck him at the base of the neck with a heavy object that made his knees buckle.

The crowd went wild with hissing and boos and at least four men drove the writer to his corner. Everyone was shouting and, dimly, he realized the gloves were being shoved over his hands. They were called skin gloves and were soft leather with very thin padding across the knuckles. Darby's broken fingers were bent and he grimaced and slapped someone aside. Order was restored and he spent a few precious seconds working those broken fingers deep into the glove. The effort was so painful that beads of sweat popped out on his forehead.

Julia and Patrick leaned through the ropes, asking what they could do.

"Nothing, now," Darby said tensely. "But if this goes past a couple of rounds, I'm going to need brandy and a pail of water. Get a sponge or towel."

"Gentlemen, come to scratch!"

Darby's corner was facing into the sun and he knew that it was no accident. Though the temperature wasn't hot, the sun was bright enough to make him squint. Patrick and Julia didn't understand ring strategy or they'd have insisted both corners be placed cross to the sun and not directed into either fighter's eyes.

They came together at the mark. Trent was a good

four inches taller and his muscles rippled. He had at least a six-inch reach advantage. As the crowd grew silent, the referee, a heavy-set, florid-faced man with red whiskers, told them the fight was to be held according to Queensbury Rules. He scowled at Darby Buckingham and said, in a low warning voice, "I've heard of you. There'll be no tripping, kicking, gouging, or any kind of foul play the likes of what you're used to under the London Rules, Buckingham. One dirty trick and you're disqualified and Mr. Trent will be the winner. Understood?"

Darby nodded and felt a sharp pain twist through his neck muscles from the unseen blow he'd taken moments earlier. He and Trent glared at each other. The tension between them was alive and the silence over the crowd seemed to tingle with expectancy. Darby flexed his powerful shoulders and his thick neck seemed to melt into his body. He was ready.

"Time!" the referee shouted and, an instant before the bell signaled, Conrad Trent unleashed a straight left jab into Darby's nose that knocked him backward.

The jab stung, but nothing more, and Darby threw a powerful right of his own that caught Trent on the shoulder and spun him halfway around. Darby moved in fast but Trent skipped away from the ropes and scored twice with that same peppering left.

At his very best, Darby had never been considered a great boxer. His attack plan was always simple and straightforward, go in swinging. Take a punch to give a harder one. Always advance and pound the will from your opponent until his mind and body succumbed to a thunderous hammering. There was no reason why he couldn't win that way now.

He plowed after Trent and threw a roundhouse right that missed and, while he was slightly off balance, Trent's fists flashed against the side of his jaw. Darby was enraged and the crowd delighted. He turned and saw Trent's mocking sneer.

"Come on, Buckingham! Show me some of that old spirit you used to have. Make a fight of it!"

Darby plodded forward. He made himself slow

down and think. No more charging after the man, because Trent had already displayed his own superior quickness. Corner the man, he told himself. Make him fight toe to toe. Yes, even at one hand to two, Darby felt he'd still have the better chance.

He cut off the ring. In short, jerking steps, he started to work Trent into a neutral corner. The man tried to dodge, but Darby anticipated his moves and shouldered him backward. Trent hit the ropes and Darby's fist blurred in a straight line, catching his opponent on the point of the jaw. Conrad's entire body stiffened and his feet left the dirt.

"Time! Time!"

Conrad Trent felt the hands pulling him erect. Somehow, he made his legs move and, just as they were about to fold, someone eased him down on a stool. He heard a roaring in his ears and wondered if it came from inside his head or from the crowd. A bottle was roughly shoved up against his teeth and he opened his mouth. Whiskey made him choke and he spit most of it out but it cleared his senses.

Roan shouted into his face and Trent leaned his head back, gasping for air.

"Boss, you can't stay with him! The man is an animal. He almost took your head off at the bell."

"He won't catch me again like that," Trent panted.

"We can't take the chance, gawddamit!"

"Time!"

Whatever else Roan had to say was lost in the shouting as Conrad left the stool and went to the mark. Surprisingly, he could think. Hadn't he taken Buckingham's famous right hand on the chin and survived? As they touched gloves and began the second round, Trent made himself concentrate on that right hand. The left was broken, he was certain of it. Watch the right! Watch the right! he kept telling himself.

Buckingham feigned with his left hoping to get him to lift his right. Trent knew better. He waited until the left was fully extended and then he countered with his own punch straight over the left and into Darby's face.

But it was like punching a tree! Buckingham merely blinked and kept pressing in. Trent found himself in a corner. He saw the murderous right hand cock back a fraction of an inch and knew it was coming.

Conrad ducked and threw his shoulder into Buckingham. Miraculously, he escaped the trap and found himself in the center of the ring.

He began to box; he quit thinking and let the old patterns of reflex fighting come back. In his college days, he'd beaten plenty of men who had better punches. He'd beaten them with quick feet and hands along with sure instincts that had always told him when to duck and bob. He was in better fighting shape than Buckingham. All he had to do was to wear him down! Stay another five rounds until the novelist's legs began to tremble under his great bulk. Then, go for him!

Trent was backpedaling furiously, dodging Buckingham's bull-like charges, jabbing with his left to the eyes. He could see them reddening. Then, he had a flash of inspiration and his spirit took wings. As Buckingham pawed outward, measuring with his useless left glove, Trent stepped back and punched it as hard as he could.

The effect was exhilarating! Buckingham's face became ashen and he saw the man's eyes dilate with pain as a groan poured from his lips. Trent would have liked to watch that pain but, in that split second of vulnerability, he came in throwing leather with both fists. His first punch caught the writer high on the forehead and staggered him, and his second pounded into the man's eye.

Buckingham tried to close the distance but Trent, having inflicted his victory, danced away, taunting, "Stick it out again, hack. Stick it out again! Show me your left!"

"Time!"

Darby Buckingham knew he was in dire trouble. He was out of shape, winded, and the single blow to his glove by Trent had splintered his two finger bones so that they grated.

"Are you . . . losing?" Julia asked.

He almost laughed. Of course he was losing! Yet, so bleak were Julia's and Patrick's expressions that he didn't have the heart to say so. "Don't count me out," he said. "The fight is young and anything can happen."

"What's the matter with your left hand, Mr. Buckingham?" Patrick asked.

"Time!"

Darby came off his stool for the third round and his expression was grim at the scratch line. In the first two rounds, he'd at least wanted to keep Trent honest by the threat of his left, now the truth was exposed and the stockbroker would strive to take advantage; he'd bang the fractured hand every chance he had. The best Darby could do was to throw his left arm up as a shield and keep Trent from picking his eyes out with the jab. There was always the off chance that Trent might crack his knuckles on the elbow if he wasn't careful, Darby thought, unleashing a whistling overhead right that missed and sent him off balance.

Trent was on him in a fury, throwing punches with both hands. Darby shoved him away and realized his vision was blurred. Trent pecked him twice more and, when he dodged away, the writer saw blood on his opponent's gloves and realized it came from his own brow. Darby couldn't feel the cut, yet knew it was deep. Trent was spotting it like a bullseye.

"Stand up and fight, damn you!"

Conrad Trent answered with his razor-sharp left and danced away as the round ended.

The crowd, perhaps sensing the end, hollered lustily.

Between rounds, Darby's head sagged down close to his knees and the blood from his forehead dripped steadily. He was out of breath and he didn't waste any in conversation.

"Time!"

As Darby ploughed forward, he knew he had to try

something desperate or the fight was already lost. Trent was too fast and sharp to floor with a roundhouse punch and he was staying out of range, pecking away with the jab and waiting for the right moment to unload.

Darby gave him the moment. He appeared to stumble under a punch and his big arms fell an inch or two.

Trent didn't need a written invitation. He had the killer instinct and was on him in savage fury as Darby continued to flounder helplessly on the ropes.

The crowd exhorted its favorite to complete the destruction and Trent answered magnificently by throwing a barrage of heavy punches until Darby was leaning on the ropes. Then, tossing caution aside, Trent set his feet to administer the knockout punch.

He never quite delivered.

Darby sprang off the rope's tension and, fearing he might miss the chin, whipped an uppercut from bootlevel that caught Trent in the stomach and lifted him six inches off the ground.

Trent screamed in agony and his eyes almost exploded from their sockets.

Darby cocked back his fist; he was going to finish the man.

"Time! Time!" the referee shrieked as he jumped between them.

The crowd was hysterical! Darby could hear them shouting with the familiar crazed blood-lust that had driven him from prizefighting a decade ago.

Trent was bent over double, his mouth was gasping for air and he was swaying badly when his friends supported him to the corner.

Darby slowly turned around. His heart was pounding wildly and for the first time, he felt confident he could win the battle. On his way back to the corner, he saw Dolly Beavers standing beside Patrick. She didn't wait for him but swept through the ropes and helped him the rest of the way.

"Darby, you're bleeding!" she cried.

His lips were puffy but he still managed to smile. "It's almost over, my dear."

She nodded, her face pale and scared. "I don't want either of you hurt anymore," she said, grabbing a towel from the water pail and sponging his eyes. "Oh, Darby, it isn't worth this!"

"It is if I beat him," Darby gritted.

"Please, stop the fight before one of you is killed! I promise I won't buy his stock if only you'll quit.

Darby shook his head. He just couldn't. And seeing that, Dolly turned and was gone. The rest period seemed to last forever as Darby stared sullenly across the ring at his opponent. They were giving him extra time and, by the look on the man's face, he needed it.

Conrad Trent knew he couldn't withstand another of Buckingham's devastating punches. In four rounds of boxing, he'd only been hit twice. Once in the first round when his jaw had almost been ripped off, and the second time just moments ago when the writer had suckered him into a mistake.

Roan whispered frantically into his ear and Trent vaguely understood. He nodded and Roan took his gloves and began sopping them with a wet sponge soaked in alkali water.

"Go for the eyes. His eyes, man! Jab this stuff into those eyes!"

Trent nodded.

"Time!"

The first jab into his eye felt like a burning poker. A red flame shot across his vision and Darby blinked rapidly to erase the stinging fury. Dimly, he knew Trent was plummeting him back into the ropes and he swung but missed.

Trent's fist blurred, then banged, and the other eye began to weep. He heard Dolly's high-pitched cry and it sounded far away. Darby stumbled forward, taking blow after blow, until he found himself across the ring and felt the ropes lace across his chest. A fist exploded against his side, just over the kidneys and Darby's knees buckled.

After all these years, he was going to be beaten. Never before had he even been knocked down for the count. But now, it was over. He couldn't see.

Another punch caught him behind the ear and Darby slumped over the ropes, trying desperately to hang on.

Suddenly, Trent grunted in pain and, very close, Darby heard young Patrick Cassidy yelling something unintelligible.

The referee and the crowd poured in on them and it was only then Darby found that the Irish boy had tackled Trent and punched him to the ground.

The fight was over. Darby Buckingham had been disqualified.

SEVEN

"Stay in your room, Mr. Buckingham. Avoid the light of day and don't forget to apply that medicine to your eyes at least every four hours."

Stretched flat out under his bed covers, Darby merely nodded without opening his eyes. He couldn't have seen much anyway, because the windows were curtained, making the room dark and gloomy.

Dr. Parker snapped his bag shut with an air of finality. "You were lucky not to lose your sight, Mr. Buckingham. Almighty lucky!"

Darby's head rose. "No, I wasn't," he said thickly, "Trent's punches didn't blind me, his gloves were treated with some vile compound or poison!"

"Maybe," the doctor admitted, "by the time I saw you, both eyes had been washed out clean. Yet, they're inflamed and scalded, I'm afraid."

"Blast!" Darby stormed. "As soon as I can see that man, I'm going to pound the life out of Trent!"

"Just as long as you do it from your bed," the doctor replied. "You need at least a week for those eyes to heal."

"Impossible!"

The doctor paused on his way out the door. "Mr. Buckingham, I'm talking about your *eyesight*. About the chance of partial blindness! It's your decision. Think it over carefully."

When the door closed, Darby slammed his fist down on the bed in anger. A week! How could he possibly remain in bed for an entire week?

"Mr. Buckingham," Patrick said firmly, "you have to do as he ordered. Besides, you wouldn't be alone."

"I wouldn't?"

"Certainly not."

"Wait a minute," Darby said, "you can't stay here. After what happened in the ring, Trent will surely be out to do you harm. And, with my eyes, I can't . . ."

"Don't worry, sir. I have a gun and . . ."

Darby sighed. Though his eyes were closed, he could detect the resolution in Patrick's voice. But it wasn't enough. If Trent hired someone to kill or harm the boy, Darby knew he would never forgive himself.

"Your offer," he said gently, "is brave and generous, but I cannot accept. Until I can figure out a way to bring Conrad Trent to his knees, the only safe place for you is . . . and it pains me deeply to say this . . . is back down in the mine. I trust McKenna and you'll have friends all around."

"But . . ."

"You must," Darby said, his words flat with conviction. "But I promise you I'll find a way to put Trent in prison. And, somehow, I'll get the Emerald Mine back in your hands."

Patrick Cassidy was quiet for a long time before he spoke again. "I'll go on one condition, Mr. Buckingham. And that's knowing there's someone here to look after you. To bring meals and keep you company."

He would need help and there was no sense in being stubborn. Darby nodded with reluctance.

"Good," Patrick said. "Miss Julia and I have already talked this over. She'll be happy to do it."

"What!"

"You won't talk her out of it and I'm not going to leave until you agree."

"Blast! I can't have that woman in here for an entire week!"

Darby had never heard Patrick Cassidy laugh and, when he did, it sounded high and boyish but straight from the heart. "Cheer up, Mr. Buckingham. Miss Julia knows how to take care of a man. She'll have you up and around in no time. Right now, she's waiting in the lobby. I'll ask her in."

Before Darby could formulate an appropriate response, he heard the door close.

During the next few moments, his mind was awhirl with all the excuses why Julia Bulette could not remain in his room as his companion. It wasn't so much a matter of reputation as the effect it would have on Dolly Beavers. Any hope that they might renew their romance would be destroyed. Julia was so well known that word of her charity would be seized by every gossip on the Comstock. Tongues would wag until hell froze over. They'd never believe she'd just nursed his health. No, he decided, in the gentlest way possible, he had to forcefully make it clear he couldn't accept her offer.

"Mr. Buckingham?"

"Come in!"

He heard her footsteps cross the floor, and the bed creaked as she sat down beside him. Darby was glad he had an excuse not to look her in the eye.

"Miss Bulette," he began.

"Why don't we start calling each other by our given names. After all, Darby, we are going to become quite familiar with one another."

"Jul-eee-ah," he said with a crack in his voice.

"Yes?" She laughed. "A bit more practice and you'll do fine."

Darby cleared his throat. "Julia, I can't allow you to stay here."

"Why not?"

"Because . . . because, I know you have a large clientele and it will cost you a great deal of money."

She chuckled gaily. "Oh, then that's the way of you, is it?"

"Yes, and . . ."

"Well you needn't worry, Darby. I've been entertaining too much lately and I need a rest, if you understand my meaning."

He understood it very well. Too well.

"Besides, there's vanity behind my offer. I think that if we become close friends, you'll be certain to put me in your next book."

"Oh, but I would anyway!"

"That's fine. What I'd like you to do is try and let people know that, while we are bad women, we do a hell of a lot of good for men."

"No question about it," he said, nodding vigorously.

"I'm not sure if I told you, but I'm one of the softest touches in Virginia City."

Darby had a thought but wisely kept silent.

"If ever one of my regular visitors gets hurt or sick or even just needs a few dollars to hold him over until he gets paid, I'll loan him the money without paper."

Darby knew this was so, for he'd had more than one man recount Julia's generosity as well as swear by her other talents.

"I'm good to the men of this city. Very good. In fact," Julia said, pride filling her voice, "the entire Virginia City Fire Company made me an honorary member in 1861, and I led them in the Fourth of July parade."

This, he hadn't heard about. "That is quite an honor."

"You'd better believe it, Darby. Some of the married firemen took a lot of steam from their wives, but they still voted me into their ranks. And I rode on top of their fire wagon carrying the company trumpet, filled with red roses brought all the way from San Francisco by the Wells, Fargo and Company. My boys pulled the wagon and marched so fancy they brought tears to people's eyes."

"I'll put it in my book, Julia." He meant it.

"Thank you." She squeezed his hand. "Also, if you have an extra page, you might tell how I turned my entire house into a hospital and became a nurse when over a hundred miners got sick from drinking bad water."

"What was wrong with it?"

"Some drunk was bitter and fed up over hard luck. Anyway, he threw a dead coyote into one of our water tanks a few years back."

Darby swallowed noisily but said nothing.

"I've got plenty of good stories like that and you'll have a chance to hear them all!" Her voice dropped. "They *should* be heard, because I'm not going to stay here forever. Last month, some of the respectable women raised such a fuss I decided to give up my orchestra seat at Maguire's Opera House and take a box in the wings."

Darby recognized the hurt in her tone. "Well, you can't let people like that bother you."

"I know," she sighed. "But it does, and I'm going to choose me someone for a husband and go to California." Julia laughed. "Maybe it's not too late to become a lady and raise a family. All it takes is the right man."

"You must have plenty of choices," he said, then felt his face warm from the realization that he'd chosen his words with less than careful forethought.

Julia, however, thought nothing of it and said, "No, I don't think it will be one of my visitors. Though some of them are fine gentlemen."

"I'm sure they are," Darby assured her, wishing he could turn the conversation in another direction.

"Like you."

"What?"

"Yes. I'd like to marry someone rich and famous. A handsome, strong fellow like yourself, Mr. Buckingham."

He was at a loss for words. Julia was a very pretty woman, but . . .

"Oh, quit squirming," she ordered. "I saw how Miss Beavers looks at you. My guess is she's already got you tethered to her pole and you don't even know it."

"Nonsense," he said stoutly, "I'm my own . . ."

A timid knock sounded at the door.

"Who is it?" Darby called.

"It's me."

"Oh, no!" he whispered, "it's Dolly!"

"My, my," Julia said, "I'm afraid this won't look too good."

"Good! This is awful!"

"Please open the door, Darby. I've come to make up."

Darby groaned. He found his eyes open but couldn't see much. "Please," he begged, gripping Julia's hand. "Do you suppose you could . . ."

"Hide?"

"Yes! I'll explain later."

"No need," Julia said with a trace of irritation. "Where do you suggest?"

"Under the bed. Quick!"

"Darby, are you all right?" There was a riding edge of anxiety in Dolly's voice now.

"Yes, fine!" he called. "I'm coming."

"Damnation," Julia swore, "I can hardly wait until you finish that story about being your own man."

Darby kicked off the covers and stumbled over her, almost falling. "Hurry."

"It's tight under here," she complained, wriggling her way under the bed.

"Shhh!"

"I'll be damned if I'll stay under here for long, Darby."

He groped wildly across the dark room and, after what seemed like an eternity, he located the door knob.

"Oh, Darby," she sobbed, throwing herself into his arms. "I don't love Conrad Trent. I'll never love anyone but you."

He tried to wrestle her out into the hallway but it was hopeless and she slipped under his arms.

"Darby, why can't we just be like we used to be? Tell me you love me and I'll never leave your side. I'll stay with you forever. I don't care if you never make poetry for me. Just take me in your arms!"

He would. He had to. Then he'd ask her to go, just long enough so that Julia might escape. He *did* want her by his side during the coming days while his eyes mended.

Darby raised his arms. He couldn't see her very well but even her perfume tasted good. Then, she threw herself at him with a cry of happiness.

Together, as always, they crashed onto the bed.

There was a muffled hoot, then a fast series of whoops like a bear going through the thickets. This culminated in a strangled cry.

"Help!"

Dolly's rapture vanished.

"Who's that!"

"No one, no one!" He tried to cup his hands over her ears but the cries only grew louder. Too late. Dolly was off the bed and Darby shoved his head under the pillow. He didn't want to know the rest.

It was short and sweet. There was nothing wrong with Dolly's eyes. She gave one squeal of womanly indignation and was gone with a crash of the door.

"You can come out from under the pillow now," Julia said heavily.

Darby hurled the pillow away. It was over! He'd never see Dolly Beavers again. In her grief and anger, she'd probably turn to Conrad Trent for support. She'd be swindled out of her money. All was lost.

"Well," Julia said, "I can see how it is. Don't blame her. Any respectable woman would have done the same. Everyone knows what I am."

Julia walked over to his bureau. "I brought you some flowers, Mr. Buckingham. I'm ... I'm sorry. I honestly meant well. Goodbye."

"Julia, wait!" He sat up and took a deep breath, then he began to speak. "What happened can't be changed. And ... and you're right. Now that I'm sure I've lost Miss Beavers, it seems pointless to deny that I loved her. I don't blame her. No more than I blame you."

He stood up and his chin lifted. "I'm a writer, Miss Bulette, and I have work to do this week. You know as much about the Comstock as anyone alive. I need your help. I want you to stay."

"But . . ." Julia Bulette swung around, gestured hopelessly toward the door as if to tell him the woman he really needed was gone.

"Over at the desk is my quill and notepad. Please get them. I can write by feel after all these years."

She wavered.

"Miss Bulette," he said patiently, "we will begin at the beginning. What Virginia City was like when you arrived. And I must warn you not to leave out your personal contributions in times of trouble. No names and no self-recriminations. Tell me your good deeds, Miss Bulette. Tell them with pride!"

A low sob was torn from her lips and Julia twisted away and Darby knew it was because she didn't want him to see her cry. After several minutes of pretending great interest in arranging her vase and flowers, Julia went to get the paper and quill.

Dolly bathed her face in cold water for a long time until she was satisfied the puffiness around her eyes was gone. Finding Julia Bulette under Darby's bed had shaken her to the core and she was in real need of some self-confidence. She knew where to get it. Conrad Trent still found her attractive.

She dressed in a manner that accentuated her small waistline and large bosom. Yet, the outfit she chose was neither flashy nor revealing. She wanted Conrad to attend to serious business. The time to invest in Emerald Mine stock was long overdue. Its price soared higher every hour and her indecision based on Darby's warning had already cost them a fair profit.

Damn that Darby Buckingham! If he found Julia Bulette's charms greater than her own, why hadn't he at least been honest enough to say so? No more playing the romantic fool. Her eyes were still puffy and a little red, but at least they were wide open.

The discovery of Julia explained so many things, she wondered why she hadn't figured it out by herself.

Julia was the reason Darby hadn't sent for her and why, after their unexpected arrival, the writer had been so unfriendly. The shock of realizing that he preferred another woman cut like a knife blade and she wasn't certain whether she'd ever fully recover. But even worse, she believed Darby's lack of honesty was the cruelest part of all. And to think she'd felt a twinge of guilt when she'd been with Conrad Trent!

No more. Conrad was rich, handsome, charming, and the finest hunk of bachelor Dolly had seen outside of Darby Buckingham. And best of all, the man wanted her, he honestly did. Dolly finished brushing her hair and then she started for the bank. She was going to withdraw the thirty thousand dollars and buy Emerald stock as Trent had advised. And after business, she was looking forward to some pleasure.

Conrad Trent smiled when he saw Dolly approach his office and, at the same instant, grimaced from the pain in his jaw. Despite the heavy application of ice bags, he knew his face was slightly disfigured from the single blow that Darby Buckingham had landed in the first round of yesterday's battle. No matter, in a couple of days he would be as handsome as ever. Besides, he reasoned, he was probably fortunate the jaw hadn't been shattered. Conrad doubted that a mule could have kicked him any harder. As a boy, he'd seen Darby knock out men before with one punch, but he'd never really appreciated the awesome power until he'd felt it in person. He'd been damn lucky to survive and actually win on the foul. Thank God for alkali water. As soon as the pandemonium broke out in the ring, his cornermen had dumped the mixture and eliminated all evidence. Conrad didn't expect Darby to pay his losses. The public victory against the ex-champion of the world was payment enough.

Besides, he thought, rising from his desk and going to meet Dolly, the final reward was walking in right now. Victory, honestly earned or not, was sweet.

"Miss Beavers! What a pleasant surprise." He

bowed, kissed her hand, and looked into her eyes. He
was surprised, then gratified. The dear woman had
shed tears of joy over his ring triumph.

"Conrad," she said, "are you all right?"

"Of course. There was never any doubt I would win.
Your friend, Mr. Buckingham, tried to batter me, but I
fought too intelligently and well. Besides, I'm obviously in superior condition."

A cloud passed across her eyes. "Mr. Buckingham is
no longer my friend. And . . . and I'd appreciate your
never mentioning his name again."

Surprise, then delight rose up inside. "Why, of
course, my dear woman. I understand."

Dolly reached into her handbag and produced a
tight bundle of money. "Thirty thousand dollars, Conrad. If you still advise, I want you to purchase Emerald stock."

He should have jumped at the money, grabbed it
from her hand, and danced with joy knowing it would
soon be his—but, for some unfathomable reason, he
did not. Perhaps it was those swollen eyes that had
shed tears over his pain. That, and the fact that her
expression was so innocent and filled with an almost
childlike trust.

"What's the matter? Has something happened to the
stock?" she asked apprehensively.

Conrad took a deep breath and whacked down the
guilt that rose inside. He *made* his hand reach out and
take the money. The feel of the crisp bills in his palm
gave him the strength he needed.

"Goodness, no! I was just . . . just wishing you'd
bought it last week as I advised. The stock has gone
through the roof these past few days."

"How much?"

Conrad pivoted and walked to his desk. He made a
pretense of shuffling through a pile of telegrams. "Ah,
here it is. Let's see." He made a clucking sound and
shook his head as though making a very difficult decision.

"Well?"

"It's still undervalued, Dolly. Today I've sent a team into the mine for new ore samples. If they grade as I expect, the stock will continue to go up."

"How much?" She came over to him and raised her chin. "Conrad, I know you feel badly that I could have bought last week at a much lower price. But that's behind me now, as are so many other things that seemed important at that time." She took a deep breath. "I'm a business woman and I respect your advice. You've already saved me from making one mistake with that awful fraud, Mr. Leroy Thomas. Now, tell me the price and I'll buy whatever amount I can."

How he admired her spunk! "Very well," he said heavily, "Emerald is going on the San Francisco Stock Market and, therefore, here in Virginia City, at one hundred ten dollars per share."

Her eyebrows lifted a fraction and he saw her reach out and steady herself against the desk as she realized it had about doubled in the week.

"How many shares for thirty thousand?"

He divided it out and said, "You can buy 272 shares."

"Then do, please."

He appeased his conscience by advising her to make it an even 270 shares. "That way you still have 300 dollars cash for living expenses."

She nodded but said nothing. He felt like a Judas.

"And I'll tell you what, Dolly. I promise to cut down on those expenses by taking you to dinner every night . . . if you like," he added, taking her hands.

Her voice was so low that Conrad could barely hear it when she said yes. And she didn't meet his eyes when he told her he'd be by to escort her out at eight o'clock.

"Dolly, are you all right?"

"I'm fine." She whirled away and hurried to the door. "I'll be ready," she called and was gone.

Conrad was puzzled, but the stack of money on his desk diverted his thoughts toward more immediate and practical considerations. He found a satchel and stuffed it inside, then locked his office and headed for the bank and the telegraph office to place the order in Miss Dolly Beavers' name.

Fortunately, there was no one else he knew in the teller's line and, when he reached the counter, he came face to face with young, pimple-faced Allen Walker.

"You did it!" the teller whispered when Trent placed the order for deposit and sale of stock. "I knew you could get her money."

He winked with lecherous delight and said, out of the corner of his mouth in a low undertone, "I bet you never had more pleasure making thirty thousand in your life!"

"Shut up," he hissed savagely. If there hadn't been bars separating them, Trent would have battered that leering expression.

Walker jerked back. His cheeks flamed as red as the pustules which marked it. "Nobody heard me," he rasped. "And I never said a word to anyone. Why are you mad?"

He looked ready to bawl and Conrad had a sudden urgency to leave before something went wrong.

"Mr. Trent, answer me!" he cried loudly enough to cause Mr. Croft, the stern countenanced bank president, to eye them.

"Get a grip on yourself!" Trent spat between locked teeth.

"I'm trying to!" Walker glanced around, saw his employer studying him critically. His ink-smudged fingers trembled as he scribbled out the bank slips for deposit. "But I *have* to know if I should still hang on to my stock until it reaches one-fifty. I've borrowed heavily. If they find out what I've done here, they'll throw me in jail. It took bank money. I've got to know!"

Conrad's anger evaporated and, in its place, there rose a malicious satisfaction. Without realizing it this detestable fellow had exposed his vulnerability and sealed his own miserable fate. He was a nuisance and, more importantly, a loose end.

"How much did you steal?" he asked quietly.

"Borrowed! I'm going to pay it back, Mr. Trent. But it must be soon or I'll be discovered!"

Trent thought quickly. "It'll go up as I said, only higher. You can make an extra fifty per share. Hang on until it reaches two hundred and then sell fast."

"But when!"

"Something wrong here, Walker?" Mr. Croft asked, his bushy eyebrows rising over his wire-rimmed glasses.

"Oh no, sir!"

The banker nodded. "Good afternoon, Mr. Trent. Please excuse Walker's ineptitude. He hasn't been himself lately. A matter that I promise will soon be rectified."

Trent grinned. "I'm afraid I'm to blame for the length of our conversation. Weather and stocks. Everyone is interested."

"Yes, of course," the banker said in a huffy voice. "But not on work time."

Allen Walker's fingers were shaking so badly he could barely hold the pen with which he was now working furiously. He shoved the paperwork forward and said, almost in a falsetto, "Come back soon, Mr. Trent. Nevada Commerce Bank always welcomes your patronage."

"Thank you and good day."

"WHEN!" There was anguish in the hushed voice.

Trent swiveled back to the cage, pretending to check to make sure he'd forgotten nothing. "One week. Sell at two hundred," he whispered tersely. Then, smiling at those in line, he made his exit.

Late that afternoon, as he was preparing to leave his office, greatly anticipating his evening with Dolly Beavers, a man popped through his door to inform him that the newest ore samples from the Emerald Mine had assayed higher than expected. Nine hundred dollars per ton! The stock was sure to go up in the morning and there'd be a crowd waiting to buy.

Trent merely nodded. He'd known what the assay report would read. He'd made sure by planting the ore two days ago. Everything was going as planned.

He fully expected his evening with Miss Dolly to go the same way. She'd, of course, hear about the promising new assayer's report. Trent laughed. The lovely woman was going to be *very* grateful.

EIGHT

With Julia at his bedside, time passed almost pleasantly for Darby Buckingham. Julia was an endless source of knowledge about the Comstock and its inhabitants. Darby listened with fascination to her stories of gallantry, determination, suffering, and even a few bizarre twists of fate that he intended to use in his book. Quirky things, her accounts, but he felt they illustrated the humor and the tragedy of a Virginia City miner. Like the one about the famous Burro Bandito, a former pack animal that had been turned loose. The wily animal became adept at sneaking through the camps late at night, devouring entire sacks of flour and cornmeal. So stealthy was the Burro Bandito that he was never apprehended and many a prospector cursed his name at daybreak and went without morning pancakes. Eventually, however, someone got even by mixing a sack of flour liberally with yeast and deliberately leaving it out one night.

They found the infamous thief two days later at a water hole. He'd apparently been plenty thirsty from his last meal but, when he drank, the yeast had begun to rise. It had inflated his belly until he looked like a balloon with toothpick legs. A gruesome ending for certain.

Darby used that story because of its ironic justice. Also ironic, but not so just, was the account Julia told of three miners who had died recently. A stray mongrel of sizable proportions had been chasing a rabbit across the hillside. Its prey came upon a working mine shaft and nimbly dodged around, but the mongrel tried to leap over the chasm. He never made it. The animal fell over two hundred feet and the impact of his body killed all three below.

So it was that, day by day, Darby's book progressed. Finally, the subject of stock markets was raised and, with it, the name of Conrad Trent.

"Trent is a crook," Julia stated flatly, "but no one has ever ben able to prove it."

Darby said nothing. The very mention of Trent raised the hackles on his neck. And when he thought about Dolly being with him, soaking up his wretched poetry and falling prey to his lies, the writer shook with cold fury.

Even worse, he was certain that, after Dolly had found Julia, she'd gone to Trent and invested all of Zack's, Bear's, and her own money. She'd probably bought at right about a hundred dollars per share; it gave him small consolation that the stock had actually risen to nearly one hundred and fifty yesterday. Remarkable. Inexplicable. Ominous.

"Are you listening to me?" Julia asked.

He hadn't been. "Oh, yes. To every word. Please, don't stop now."

Julia eyed him skeptically but went on. "I was saying that your ex-friend had better watch out for Mr. Trent."

Darby was all ears now; he sat straight up in the bed and his eyes were open. "Why?"

"Why? I just told you!"

"Tell me again."

"Because," Julia said patiently, "I've heard that Conrad Trent is a bigamist."

"What!"

"Take it easy, Darby."

He couldn't, and grabbing Julia by the shoulders, he pulled her close. "Tell me everything you know about him. The bigamist part, I mean."

Julia's dark brown eyes dipped to each of her shoulders, where his hands rested. She smiled. "What's the matter? Does the idea of bigamy excite you?"

"Of course not!" He released her, saw disappointment, and guessed he was being too unfair and impatient. She'd been very good to him. Not as good as he felt she would like to be, but good enough for respectable purposes.

"This bigamy thing," he said, leaning back on the pillow. "It just might be the way to bring Trent down."

"I doubt it. Some of the girls . . . my associates in the profession . . . have had Trent as a client. Though not since Miss Beaver's arrival, I'm afraid."

Darby stiffened. Clenched his teeth. "Go on."

"Well, there's not really much to tell. Only rumors that Trent has been married at least twice and that his latest wife is some poor innocent young thing in San Francisco."

"Her name! What's her name?"

Julia actually blushed. "I shouldn't say this, but, once in a while, after Trent has had a few drinks too many, and he's . . . shall we say, enjoying the highlight of his visit . . ."

"For God's sake, Julia! I don't care about the details. What name does he call?"

"Names. There are more than one. The latest is named Suzette. Before her there was Caroline."

Darby was aghast. Shocked and outraged. "How can you be certain that, in a moment of passion, he isn't just reliving old affairs?"

"Because he never visits unless he is very drunk and that isn't often. But, one time or another, he's said he has their copper-plate daguerreotypes framed and in his office desk drawer. Suzette and Caroline."

"Together?"

"Don't be ridiculous. He may get drunk but never so bad he'd admit to bigamy. No," Julia said with perfect conviction, "the admissions and the evidence were given to separate associates of mine on two different occasions. Us professionals aren't accepted by women outside the trade, so we stick together. You know, compare notes, help each other over troubles, pass the word about which men like to get rough."

Darby started to get up.

"You can't leave. The doctor said . . ."

"Never mind what he said. I've got to warn Dolly."

"Wait a minute," Julia protested. "What I've just told you is confidential. If you go accusing Conrad Trent, he may remember my friends and hurt them."

"I can't just stand by and let him mislead Dolly!"

"What else can you do? If you accuse the man, he'll deny it. Get rid of those pictures. Then he'll punish my friends. Oh Darby, please!"

Darby flopped back down. She was right, dammit. "Get a bottle of brandy out of the cabinet," he said. "This calls for some serious thinking. Maybe if we put our heads together on it, we can divine *some* way to expose the truth. We've got to."

The hour was late and it eventually took most of two bottles of Darby's imported brandy before they hit upon the plan. It was bold and involved a great deal of personal risk, yet there seemed to be no other way. A drunken man, to Darby's way of thinking, would not invent imaginary wives nor brag of keeping their daguerreotypes in his office. If they could be found, perhaps Dolly would finally realize Trent's real character.

Darby filled their glasses once more and eyed Julia, who was now looking uncommonly pretty. "Besides," he said with relish, "even if we are caught, it will give me the chance to settle the matter of who is the better man. No poisons, no corrupt ring officials. Just myself and Mr. Trent. That, dear Julia, is the way it should have been from the start."

She giggled and made a big show of testing his mighty biceps. When she suggested that perhaps they should wait until the night was just a little bit further along, Darby caught her understanding but declined. It wasn't easy, though. Julia, pretty at any hour, was fast becoming a ravishing beauty. It was time to leave, while he still could. As she was going, Julia produced a hip flask from her skirts and filled it to ward off the night's chill. Darby smiled tolerantly. His cheeks were flushed with excitement. The thought of combat was enough to keep his blood circulating.

Conrad Trent had not wanted to leave Dolly Beavers. He couldn't remember when he'd been more enamoured by a woman. Oh, Suzette was as lovely, and a bit younger, yet she was always so reserved and proper.

After dinner they'd gone to the opera house and seen a farcical comedy entitled Mother's Helper. Nonsense, really, but it had seemed to lift Miss Beaver's spirits and set the tone for a late night intimacy at the Crystal Club.

He'd really perked her up with the news about the Emerald stock advance, yet...yet, somehow, she'd eluded his suggestion they share one last drink together in the privacy of his home. Dammit, anyway! Tomorrow night, he'd win her for sure.

Trent, always confident, had a smile on his face when he reached his door. But, as soon as he unlocked it and saw a trace of light dance far down the hallway, his smile evaporated and every nerve in his body jangled with alarm. He drew his gun and stepped inside. In almost total darkness, he tiptoed down the hallway and flattened himself against the wall. Then, he heard their voices.

"Hold the candle closer, Julia."

A whisper, but instantly recognizable as belonging to none other than Darby Buckingham.

"Look! It reads: to my dearest husband, Suzette Trent."

"And here!" Darby hissed, "this other one is just as good: Love always, your faithful wife, Caroline. What a poor, innocent fool!"

"Let's go, Darby. You've got what you want."

Trent heard footsteps across the carpet. He sped lightly down the black hallway until his fingers touched the ascending stairway. Then, he ducked under it and waited, feeling trapped in a dilemma. He had no desire to kill either of them, but dammit, he couldn't let them escape with those pictures. There was only one real alternative and Trent reversed the heavy Navy Colt in his fist and silently raised it. When they stumbled by, he made no mistake and his arm rose and fell with stunning force. Buckingham toppled on the candle and Julia's scream filled the hallway, but died in her throat as he knocked her unconscious.

It was shortly before dawn when he and Roan finally lowered them down to the bottom of the Emerald mine shaft. Roan had wanted to crush in their heads with a rock but Trent hedged. Murder wasn't his style. Had the fact been known, Quinn Cassidy was the first man he'd ever killed and that had been a matter of self defense.

"Boss, listen! We've got no choice! It's them or us." His eyes narrowed. "We don't even have to kill them."

"What the hell do you mean? If . . ."

This was Roan's area of expertise and he seemed to take charge. "Julia and this Buckingham are too popular to shoot. That would raise a big stink. So we leave them down here and let nature take its course. We knock the bottom half of the ladder apart and cover the shaft with tin. In this temperature and without water they won't last two days."

"You mean just let them die of thirst?"

"It's either that or kill them."

He nodded. There wasn't any choice. It was a matter of survival. "All right," he said tiredly. "After they're dead I'll authorize the completion of a new assay report and those two will be discovered. Everyone will think they died in the fall and . . ."

His entire body stiffened as though he'd been jolted by lightning. "That's it!"

"What?"

"Our story, man! I'll throw a sack of high grade ore down the shaft. Then, when Buckingham and Julia are found, we can say *they* were salting the mine all along. But this time, the ladder broke and they fell to the bottom and died."

Roan nodded his head but without enthusiasm. "I sure wanted to even the score personally with Buckingham. I ain't forgetting what he did to me up on C Street. Besides . . ."

"Besides nothing! Don't you see? This makes Buckingham the scapegoat. When the story reaches town, Emerald stock will plummet. But instead of hating me . . ."

"They'll blame Julia and Buckingham!"

"That's right," Trent said quietly. He stared down at the two crumpled figures and his mouth twisted. "The fools! They wouldn't leave well enough alone. And now . . . now their deaths offer me the perfect irresistible solution."

Roan smiled cruelly. "They'll die of thirst down there. No one will hear their voices and, after a day without water, they won't be able to do much more than whisper. Boss, I want to be the one who stands guard."

"Thought you might. Keep the shaft covered and don't let anyone within a hundred feet of its opening. It's valuable property and the order won't be questioned. But you'll have to stand guard twenty-four hours a day."

"That's okay by me. I'll sleep right over there in that clearing. Right close up by the hole. No one can get by. Just send food, water, and whiskey. I'll make out."

"That's fine, Roan. But before I say yes, I want you to give me an honest answer."

In the pale moonlight, he saw Roan blink.

"Sure, boss."

"Why do you want to do this?"

Roan took a long time forming his reply but, when it came, Trent knew it was the truth.

"I heard dying of thirst is a tough way out. Mighty slow and painful. I'd kind of like to know how bad it is. I'll be listening."

Trent shuddered violently. For a moment, he almost lost his stomach for the entire plan. If he could have bribed or threatened Julia or Darby into silence he'd ᵃve done so in an instant. But that would never work. ᵗ was survival and there was no turning back now.

"I'll take the wagon back home. You get started on the bottom half of that ladder. Don't just pull the rungs loose—bust 'em!"

"Yes, sir. It'll get done right."

He started to leave, checked himself. "Roan, I hit them hard. Real hard. They might not even regain consciousness and I hope they don't. But if it happens and they start to suffer, you go down and finish them merciful so it looks like an accident."

"Dammit boss! I told you why I wanted to stay."

Trent grabbed him by the collars and jerked him up to his toes. "We're people, not savages! Not torturers! You do as I say or by God I'll reckon with you!"

He released the man. "When they're dead let me know. Immediately. I'll bring over some high grade and a shotgun so there'll be no mistake these two were trying to salt the mine. Afterward, I'll send in an assay team that will discover the bodies and the planted ore. I want the news to come from them, not us."

He hurried away then, wanting to have the wagon and team unharnessed before fire touched the sky. He didn't want to think about Darby Buckingham and Julia anymore. Perhaps he would find escape in writing poetry—the kind best remembered in the works of Edgar Allan Poe.

Because he awoke slowly and in total darkness, it was a long time before Darby fully realized the seriousness of his plight. The air was very warm and heavy with the smell of earth. It, and the throbbing pain in his head, made sleep seem infinitely preferable and so he eased back and dozed fitfully.

Darby might have continued to sleep had it not been for the low moaning that drove him back into wakefulness. At first, the sound was an annoyance but, after several minutes, it brought him upright with fear.

He groped, touched the rock about him, and shook his head as though trying to awaken from a dream without imagery or light. Darby rolled to his hands and knees and scuttled toward the sound. His fingers touched the soft body and Julia cried out in alarm.

"It's me. Darby Buckingham! Julia?"

The voice sounded drugged. "Yes . . . yes. Where are we?"

Darby fumbled through his coat pockets until he located his cigar case and matches. He jammed a Cuban between his teeth and struck a light. It sprang to life and bounced off the cold rock walls which crowded in on them. He saw a pick with a busted handle, several empty bean cans, a hammer, drills, a box with a puddle of wax which had been a candle. The flame grew hot on his fingers and Darby lit his cigar as the match burned skin, then tossed the match to its extinction.

"We're in a mine shaft," he said, inhaling deeply. In the blackness, the familiar aroma and taste of the cigar steadied his nerves and even the glowing tip seemed a comfort.

Julia groaned. "We're going to die here."

Darby crawled over to where he'd seen the box and candle. After several moments of exploration, he located the wick. By feel, he determined there wasn't more than a quarter inch of it remaining, but he puffed rapidly on his cigar until it was glowing, flicked the ash from its tip and lowered it to the wick. It took only seconds before the candle spluttered to life and, though its output was feeble, the glow illuminated their pit.

Julia's head was down and her long black hair hung tangled and lifeless about her face. Darby crawled to her side and put his arms around her, then spoke gently and with more confidence than he felt.

"We're not going to die here, Julia. There's a ladder nearby and, though it's been broken apart, we'll figure out some method of repair."

She raised her head, forced a smile that hurt him to watch. "I shouldn't have said that. I'm sorry. We have to be resourceful. Brave. But my head, it aches so bad and I don't feel at all brave."

"Nor do I," he confided. "But we'll still get out of this mess alive. I promise."

He moved over to the ladder. There was no telling

how long the candle would last and he had to make the best use of his time.

Each rung was broken in the center. A pair of two by fours like giant stilts was all that remained and, as far as the light held, he saw no rungs between. The ladder had been rickety to begin with. It might have sufficed for a boy or a very slightly built man, but it would never have supported Darby's massive weight.

His idea was to pull the sides close together, no more than a foot apart. That way, he could renail the busted rungs and hope that Julia might be able to make a start upward to where a faint slice of daylight beckoned from what seemed like a stellar distance.

Quickly, he retrieved the hammer and began straightening the square headed nails. Julia helped him lay the splintered rungs in a line and he drove nails into each side. Then, as the candle flickered dangerously, he scrambled over to the rails and tried to pull them together.

They wouldn't close and he swore. Of course they wouldn't! The upper rungs held the ladder apart. Darby slumped back, his mind racing. "Julia, see if you can rebuild the candle. Push the wax together while it's soft. Fashion a new wick. Hurry!"

There had to be a way! Think! This wasn't some western dime novel he'd written to put his hero in danger. This was himself, Darby Buckingham, and there would be no last minute heroics. Think!

Darby puffed rapidly. He could start a fire out of the busted rungs. The pit had a small cavern dug off on one side. They could huddle there and hope that the rising smoke would bring rescuers before its gases asphyxiated them.

Too risky.

The ladder. It was the only way. He picked up a rung and examined it closely as though the stubby piece of wood might provide the answer.

It did.

"I've got it!" He began to pull the nails out and redrove them through the center. Darby centered it over one of the ladder's legs and nailed it tight. He gripped it with both hands and tested its strength.

"Will it hold?"

"It must," Darby gritted, adding more rungs until he could reach no further. "You can stand on my shoulders, and I'll stand on the box. Between us, we can go at least fifteen feet."

"Then what?" Julia asked quietly. "As far as we can see, there's nothing."

"Maybe . . . maybe just beyond the light, the rungs are still in place. It's all we've got. We have to try. I'll prepare more rungs to hand up."

His urgency seemed to inspire Julia Bulette. "I found an open sardine can. I'm going to scrape all the puddled wax and use these threads from my skirt for a wick. They should work, if I first coat them with wax."

"Good!"

Confidence rose in his chest. They *were* going to lick this. To think about revenge against Conrad Trent would have been a luxury at that moment, one he couldn't afford. Every bit of his mind and concentration had to focus on their escape. But afterward . . .

"Are you ready?"

"Yes."

"Place your foot in my cupped hands. As soon as you go up, take hold of the sides. I'll hand you the hammer and nails."

Julia brushed back her hair. The new candle was much brighter and he could see her face clearly when she spoke. "We *are* going to make it," she said staunchly. "Once, when I was a little girl, we built a tree house. It wasn't much. Couldn't have been more than six or seven feet off the ground. But we nailed a ladder just like this one and, though I was scared witless at first, I made it up."

"And you will now. Here, give me your foot."

"Don't rush me, Darby Buckingham. I'm feeling like that small girl all over again. Only this time, it's so much higher and if I fall . . ."

"Then I'll catch you, Julia. I swear I'll catch you in my arms."

"Show me how. Please."

Darby unlaced his cupped fingers and straightened. Julia's face was smudged with dirt and there was a smear of dried blood on her cheek. He didn't see any of it. She looked, in that moment, very brave and heartachingly vulnerable. He wrapped her into his arms and kissed her long and deeply as she clung to him for support and courage.

His lips brushed over her shuttered eyes and he whispered, "When you were that little girl, you didn't have me to catch you. I won't fail. These arms won't let that happen. Now, let us begin."

With a slow upward lift, he raised Julia. Her weight was less than a hundred and twenty pounds and Darby performed the motion effortlessly.

She stood on his shoulders and reached into her skirt pocket for the hammer. Something fell out and clanked loudly on the rock floor. He glanced down and saw it was her flask.

"I'm ready. Give me the first piece of wood."

When Julia climbed past his shoulders, Darby hurried to the makeshift candle and raised it at arm's length.

"How's it going?" he called anxiously.

"It's not easy trying to hang on and strike at the same time, but I'm making progress."

"Excellent! Just be careful. Be absolutely certain each rung is solidly nailed."

Darby was filled with pride in the way Julia was handling herself. It was slow work and he knew she'd have to come down soon for more wood and to rest, but she *was* going to make it. Already she was at least twenty-five feet up.

"I see them!" she cried. "Darby, the rungs are no more than ten feet beyond my reach."

"Come down and rest."

"No! Throw me more. I can do it."

He stooped to pick up another piece of wood and

that's when he heard the sound of scraping tin from high above. Light flooded down the shaft. Julia, suspended almost a quarter of the way up, hung in the blinding orb of sunlight.

"Nice try down there," floated a mocking voice. "Sorry."

The ladder began to shake. Darby roared in frustration and yelled for Julia to come down as he gripped the stilt legs and tried to hold them steady.

It was impossible. At the surface, the ladder was yanked away from the wall and slammed over to the opposite side. Wood splintered and Julia dropped screaming as Darby lifted his arms and braced himself for the impact.

Her momentum buckled his legs until his knees struck rock. But Darby's arms held and, true to his word, Julia Bulette did not touch the ground.

He cradled her body while she trembled with shock. From up above, laughter rippled down as the tin scraped across the hole, blotting out daylight like an eclipse of the sun.

For the first time, Darby Buckingham thought of death.

NINE

The taunting from above had ended a long time ago; Darby and Julia crouched in sightless silence. Their candle was dead and so was hope. Both knew there was no chance of escape and, because of Darby's supposed convalescence, they wouldn't even be missed until the week's end. By then, it wouldn't matter. They were dehydrated, past hunger, and almost out of time.

Darby supposed their bodies were to be found and circumstances would indicate they'd fallen to their deaths because of the broken ladder. He didn't understand why Trent hadn't just thrown them both down the shaft and gotten it over with. But that would have been too humane and, clearly, the laughter from above indicated a sick and demented mind.

Still, Darby was a fighter and so was Julia Bulette. They'd hang onto life until it was torn from them. They'd survived until now only by strict rationing of the brandy, yet it was almost gone. The temperature was at least ninety-five degrees and that meant they were quickly losing body fluids. The alcohol burned their throats and made them sweat; Darby dreamed of fresh, cold water and thought, should he live, he'd never again enjoy brandy.

Tin scratched across the shaft opening high above and the waterfall in Darby's mind dried up and was gone. He opened his eyes and tried to gather his senses while Julia slept on. Far above, there was a round glow of light almost like the sun, only weak and sputtering.

It took him several seconds to realize it was a candle's flame in the night.

"Hey!" a voice drifted down to him. "I ain't heard nothing in a day and a half. You folks alive?"

Darby waited in expectant silence. His pulse began to quicken and every nerve in his body pounded to its beat.

"You gotta be dead by now," the voice answered itself.

A moment later, gravel began to cascade down the shaft and Darby edged in deeper, until he was pressed tightly against the cutback wall and as far from the ladder as he could be. Something hissed through the air and slapped the rock floor. Darby groped outward, moving silently until he touched rope. Then, as he scurried back, the ladder began to protest an added weight.

Someone was coming!

Darby fumbled around for a moment until he was absolutely certain he could feel Julia's breath on his cheek. Then, he gently closed his hand over her mouth and whispered, "Julia. Wake up. Someone's coming. Don't make a sound."

She jerked fitfully and he repeated the instructions. Julia nodded and he released the pressure. The sound of footsteps on the ladder's rungs changed to a scraping of rock; Darby knew the man was past the unbroken ladder rungs and descending all the way. He gathered his legs under him. Boots thudded on the rock floor. A match scraped. Into its yellow glow he sprang like a cornered cat.

Roan's face was momentarily illuminated and it was a mask of terror. Darby crashed into him and all was blackness again. A gun clattered on stone. There was a thud and a strangled cry, and then a primordial roar from Darby's mouth. Something beat like trapped wings against the rock floor, then slowed to a flutter, and several minutes later died in silence.

Darby made his fingers release the throat and he sagged away and tried to regain composure. In all his years of fighting, he'd never killed barehanded, like a

savage. He could have subdued the intruder, but the
insane laughter had affected him too deeply. So he'd
strangled and, given the circumstances, he guessed he
would again.

Five hours later, the passengers on the westbound
stage to Carson City, Sacramento, and San Francisco
never suspected that the handsome, though pale and
drawn, couple who boarded in Gold Hill had just been
resurrected. Both were well-dressed but very quiet.
Julia wore a dark veil, Darby was in his customary
black, and they were judged to be on their way
to a funeral, a subject which discouraged conversation.

The coach rolled through Devil's Gate into Silver
City. The hour was very early; there were no additional
passengers and the two on board disembarked, one
saying, "Whoever it was, he's in the hands of God
now."

Darby merely looked at the gentleman. Words could
not fairly express where Conrad Trent would be in the
very near future. The coach lurched forward and the
writer put his arm around Julia.

"Are you sure you are up to this trip?"

"Yes. We must, though I realize your doubts," she
replied. "And don't worry, we'll find Mrs. Trent and
I'll talk her into returning. A respectable woman would
never have accompanied you alone back to Virginia
City."

"It galls me to leave now," Darby said tightly. "I
should have hunted Trent down and killed him."

"We've been over that, Darby. Without proof that
he was behind this, you'd be railroaded by a partisan
jury—just like they did in the ring. You couldn't take
the chance."

"I would anyway, except that Dolly and the others
would suffer the loss of their fortunes. They'd never get
a dime out of Trent's estate."

"That's a certainty." Julia leaned over to rest her
head on his shoulder. "Why don't you try to get some
sleep."

Darby reached into his coat and pulled out Julia's flask. He drank deeply of its water but knew he couldn't sleep. He'd seen enough blackness and his eyes wanted to devour the sunlit mountains and rugged country.

The Sierra Nevadas rose like a jagged blue-green hedge to the sky. They were awesome in size and, beyond their heights, lay the fertile California valleys and, even beyond those, San Francisco. He'd always been interested in seeing it but this trip was not a sightseeing tour. They had one purpose only and that was to find Suzette Trent and bring her back to the Comstock before her husband bankrupted its citizens.

And they'd do it. Do it if it meant pounding on every door in San Francisco. They *had* to find that woman and quickly. There was no other choice.

Conrad Trent held another match aloft in his shaking hands and cursed the day Roan Corley was born. How! How could the man have been so stupid as to let Julia and Buckingham escape while getting himself killed? It seemed impossible. Yet, as the match flickered toward extinction, he knew the answer. Roan's viciousness and morbid curiosity had lured him to his death.

The match scorched his fingertips and Conrad tossed it away and hunkered down in the blackness to think, a sawed-off shotgun held forgotten in one fist. What he decided in the next few minutes would determine his future. The simplest solution was to tie a rope around the corpse and pull it to the surface. With any luck at all, he could have discovered elsewhere in the morning.

Yet, that wouldn't cause the Emerald Mine stock to plunge and, therefore, was unsatisfactory.

Buckingham and Julia were, of course another factor to worry about, but they'd be hard pressed to get anyone to believe what really happened. After all, their story would have to begin by admitting they'd entered his home to steal. No, he decided, neither one of them had actually seen him in that hallway. So Buckingham's hands were tied and his story was shot full of holes. Conrad dismissed them from the equation.

Suddenly, he snapped his fingers in the blackness and grinned. He would keep to his original plan only, instead of everyone thinking Julia and Buckingham had salted the mine, let them think it was Roan! Why not? He'd just claim his own employee had double-crossed him.

Conrad laughed out loud. He kicked the sack of high grade over beside the body. Next, he lit another match, broke the shotgun open and loaded the shells he'd prepared earlier that morning. He'd resorted to an old trick by filing minted coins into shavings and re-placing lead shot with U.S. silver. By firing into the right places many a wily prospector had made his fortune and the unsuspecting buyer was said to have been "silver shot."

He loaded the gun and placed it down near the body. Let them find the evidence. A sack of high grade and a modified shotgun would convince anyone that Roan died attempting to salt the mine and con the people of Virginia City into thinking it was rich. Emerald stock would plunge to nothing.

Satisfied, Trent took off his coat and brushed all the footprints away. He picked up every burnt match and trace of habitation he could find. He wasn't worried, the discovery by tomorrow's assay crew would be so startling no one would think to question his first impressions.

Conrad grabbed the rope and scrambled up with the grace of a twenty-year-old. Once on top, he left the tin pulled aside, the way Roan would have, and then he struck out for his home. Tomorrow was going to be a very interesting day.

As he walked, he remembered a few weeks back, when he'd told Roan why he'd used all the stock profits to buy heavy mining equipment. It was now in San Francisco, to be held until he ordered it delivered to the Emerald Mine. Roan had been dumbfounded and convinced that the best thing to do was to take the profits and run before someone figured things out.

Conrad believed that was the difference between someone who was content with small gains and a man like himself who had enough confidence to become wealthy. Roan had been small and mean. Now he was dead, and Conrad figured to keep the machinery and use it in the Emerald Mine. He wanted ownership and the silver fortune it would bring. Nothing less would do.

The discovery of Roan's body caused an explosion of outrage even among the few who were not stockholders. The body and the damning evidence was hoisted to the surface and a huge throng gathered on the slopes of Sun Mountain.

When they broke and marched for town, Conrad saw them coming and, despite his well-laid plans, his fingers trembled as he reached into his desk drawer and produced the machinery receipts. Each was dated and stamped, PAID IN FULL, DELIVERY GUARANTEED TO EMERALD MINE, VIRGINIA CITY, NEVADA.

Conrad heard the furious mob as they rounded the corner and marched down C Street yelling his name. Someone called for a hanging. It took every ounce of self-control he possessed not to bolt out the back door. Maybe, if there'd been a fair chance of escape, he would have. But escape from Virginia City was impossible, so he waited. Waited, knowing that life or death rested squarely on his own presence of mind and dramatic ability to make the crowd listen. His story was flawless and on his desk were eighty thousand dollars of receipts to prove he was innocent. He had only to make them listen before someone found the hanging rope.

Very carefully, Conrad stacked the pile of receipts on his desk and headed toward the front office door. He squared his broad shoulders, checked to make certain his tie wasn't crooked, then stood ready to face the people of Virginia City.

When he stepped onto the boardwalk, the crowd looked murderous. Conrad let his eyes widen with disbelief as a man shouted out the recent discovery. He took a faltering back step and leaned against the porch railing as their words assaulted him. He did his best to look as if some terrible fate had mysteriously befallen him.

"We was robbed!"

"Yeah. Your man Roan salted the goddam mine! Here," a man raged, "we found these beside his body. A sack of high grade and a shotgun filled with shot—silver shot!"

"He was your man, Trent. You put him up to it!"

They started to surge at him and Conrad knew words wouldn't stop them in time. He yanked his gun up and leveled it in the nearest face.

"You'll hear me out or some of you up front are going to die."

That stopped them for a moment.

He was about to speak when he saw a jostling in the crowd and recognized Dolly Beavers and her two partners shoving forward. The two buckskin-clad men who cleared the way to him were awesome. They carried long buffalo rifles and they appeared capable of using them.

Dolly pushed up from C Street and her eyes were filled with doubt. "Conrad, please, it can't be true."

"It isn't. I can explain."

"At the end of a rope!" a voice railed.

Dolly spun around. "Listen to him! Give Mr. Trent a chance," she cried. "Me and my partners have thirty thousand dollars invested in Emerald stock and a hanging will get us nothing."

Bear Timberly and Zack Woolsey posted themselves at her side. Their rifles were primed and ready.

"You best have a good explanation," Zack hissed, "or I'm going to pull the rope on you myself."

Conrad's mouth went dry and his first words sounded strange to his own ears.

"Gentlemen," he rasped, lifting his arms for silence. "I . . . I cannot blame you for wanting to see me hang. I'm the one who believed in that mine with all my heart."

His admission was a calculated gamble and it paid off. They hadn't been expecting that and, in the momentary confusion, he lowered his arms theatrically, palms up, to the gaping mob. The gesture was eloquent beyond words.

"I'd like to show you something, my friends. Something I'm sure that none of you are aware of." With that, he pivoted into the office to emerge a moment later with the stack of receipts.

"Pass them around, Dolly," he shouted so that everyone could hear.

"These are receipts for mining equipment I bought and paid for with my own funds. You miners will recognize what I ordered. Hoists, explosives, tools, a new steam engine of the latest design, mine cable, a dressed-pine windlass, and eight thousand feet of timber for square setting. On the receipts, you'll also see everything is to be delivered to the Emerald Mine. Bought and paid for, gentlemen! My total investment is over eighty thousand dollars."

He paused to let the impact soak in, to let the uncertainty eat into their brains. "You see, I still own two hundred and fifty shares that I bought from Quinn Cassidy. Using that stock, I borrowed heavily to finance the machinery we'd need to make the Emerald Mine pay handsomely. Would I spend eighty thousand dollars knowing the mine was salted?"

Every face in the crowd avoided his eyes. His voice cracked and he had to clear his throat of emotion. "It . . . it was to be the first real mining operation owned—not by the rich San Francisco stock men—but by *you* and me, the working citizens of Virginia City!"

Someone cursed, but there was no anger in it, only bitter disappointment.

Dolly reached out and took his hand. Conrad forced a brave smile, then pivoted back to the silent crowd. "The fault is mine, gentlemen. As you say, Roan Corley was in my employ and I should have realized he was salting. Roan's investment was substantial and he had plenty to gain. Now . . . now, it appears we've all lost."

"No!" a voice cried. "I don't believe it!"

Conrad Trent's head jerked up and, at the rear of the crowd, he saw Allen Walker. The young bank teller's face was scarlet and twisted with disbelief.

"I'm sorry," Trent called, then turned to ignore the outburst. "Some of you have lost heavily, though none as much as I. But I'll make one promise."

He seemed to straighten, grow taller and he pointed at the receipts being passed about. "That equipment is on its way over the Sierras. When it arrives, I'll sell it for as much as I can. And every dollar I take in, I'll return to you by purchasing back your worthless stock. It's a matter of personal honor."

This caused a low murmur, then excited chattering.

"How much, Mr. Trent? Some of us bought in just a few days ago. We had to pay over a hundred and fifty dollars a share."

"I know," he sighed. "Obviously, I want to spread what money I can get as evenly as possible. So I can't pay much. Ten, maybe twenty dollars a share, and that's the limit I'm afraid."

Allen Walker started babbling incoherently and a pair of men, eager to strike out at anything in their frustration, knocked him senseless. But there were others who also felt Trent's offer was less than generous.

"We can't take that kind of loss!"

"No! That's only ten or twenty cents on the dollar," another seconded.

"Gentlemen," Trent said, "there is one alternative and that is for you to keep your stock. It's possible the Emerald does contain rich ore far underground."

"Without machinery, we'll never find it," a burly Welshman proclaimed.

Trent nodded. "That's true. The choice is yours. But we can't have it both ways. I either keep or sell the machinery. If I keep it, you *may* get nothing. If I sell ... I think I can guarantee you at least twenty dollars a share."

Violent discussion erupted in small knots all around. Conrad heard Dolly telling her partners they should hang onto the stock. From what he could separate out of the others, to a man they wanted to recoup whatever they could get and be done with it—they wanted out. Conrad felt the sweat pop out across his chest. They had no idea that the Emerald Mine was valuable. He wanted their stocks before they changed their minds.

He spotted the president of his bank. "Mr. Croft!" he yelled over the arguing mass. "Have you had a chance to look over those receipts?"

"Of course," came the stiff reply. "I'm the one who advised you to go ahead and buy."

"Is it good equipment? Worth every dollar paid?"

The banker tugged at his spectacles. He wasn't at all sure why he'd been singled out for attention and his face wore a guarded look. "Yes," he said after a moment, "I'd say you bought astutely."

"Then, Mr. Croft, I'm asking you, for the sake of these good people, many of whom are your loyal depositors, to loan me the eighty thousand dollars face value of that machinery. Today. Right now. Do it, sir, and they'll long remember that, in their darkest hour, the Nevada Bank of Commerce stood with them!"

Croft blinked. Around him, the stockholders waited expectantly. He was trapped.

"Mr. Croft?" Trent asked, "the future of these people and your bank awaits your decision."

Croft mopped his face, cleaned his spectacles and perspired freely under the crowd's gaze. At last, he put on his eyeglasses and said, "When the machinery arrives, I'll have it inventoried, then impounded as collateral for your loan, Mr. Trent. That's the best I can do. These delivery dates are only a week or so away and once the machinery is inventoried, I'll make the loan. Meanwhile, I will call upon our bank reserves and make sure the funds are in order."

That satisfied the crowd, but Conrad saw Allen Walker leap to his feet, then stumble into a run. Trent wondered how much he'd dipped into the reserves. Probably not too much, but by next week Allen Walker would be on his way to prison—or dead—depending on who caught him first.

"You heard Mr. Croft! He's prepared to loan me the currency," Trent bellowed. "When the money is in my hands, I'll buy your stock on a first come, first served basis as long as my funds allow."

He grabbed Dolly by the arm as he passed. "You and your friends have priority."

"No," she said quickly.

"What do you mean!"

"I mean we paid thirty thousand dollars and can't afford to sell it back for only five or six thousand. We worked too many years to lose so much."

"I know you did," Trent whispered, "all three of you. But . . . but speculating on stock is a gamble. You have to accept the losses with the gains. My advice is to take your loss and hope for better fortune next time."

Bear stepped forward aggressively. "Your advice stinks," he rumbled. "I'm thinking we should have listened to Darby Buckingham all along."

"Amen," Zack added solemnly. "Reckon it's time we hunted him up and cleared the air."

"Dolly! Surely you don't feel the same way."

She wavered then said, "No, not really. I know you had our interests in mind. But perhaps we should have listened to him. No matter. It's too late now. He's preoccupied with other . . . things."

"May I see you this evening?" he asked as the two hunters glowered menacingly.

"You'd better. I'm feeling very poor."

Conrad raised her chin. "Don't worry," he said, "I'll see you're taken care of."

Dolly stiffened. "Don't get any fancy ideas, Conrad. I'm used to taking care of myself, thank you!"

After she left, Conrad smiled grimly. Give her time, he thought. When the loan came through, he was going to buy back the Emerald Mine stock and make a fortune.

Every map of the Comstock Lode that he'd been able to get his hands on shouted that fact. Even the true assay reports indicated that, in the last few feet, the silver value alone had gone up forty dollars a ton.

Before the first piece of mining machinery was sold, he'd strike pay dirt. In six months, he'd be the first Silver King of Virginia City. Sometime afterward, there'd probably be a fury the likes of which the Comstock had never seen when the investors realized his game. But by then, he'd be the absentee and sole legal owner and they could howl until hell froze over as far as he was concerned.

Maybe he'd take the money and go to Europe. Perhaps, if Miss Beavers displayed the full measure of her charms . . . he might just take her along. And, even if she didn't there was always Suzette waiting over in San Francisco. She was his by marriage and every bit as lovely as Miss Dolly. Either way, it would be pleasant.

TEN

San Francisco. Darby and Julia disembarked from the Sacramento River steamer and took a deep breath of the salty and refreshing Pacific Ocean breeze. Since they were traveling light, it took only a few minutes for their bags to be packed aboard a waiting coach and they were off. The driver traveled briskly along Montgomery Street, then headed toward Portsmouth Square where Julia recommended the elegant Parker House.

Darby was impressed by the size and amount of activity in this port of trade. And, although he'd never been here before, he knew its rich history very well.

San Francisco had blossomed overnight with the discovery of gold at Sutter's Creek in 1848. The news of the great find had caused a worldwide migration to this place. Darby well-remembered the alarm on the East Coast when entire communities were uprooted under the influence of gold fever. Some had gone overland, even more had undertaken the perilous voyage through the Straits of Magellan and around the Horn. So great was the urgency, many had sailed away on rotting, unseaworthy vessels and had never been heard from again.

Thousands, however, had made it. Landing on these very shores, they'd launched themselves at the Sierras with fevered eyes that blazed with the quest for gold. Few had ever realized riches, not even Sutter or the discoverer, James Marshall. By 1860, the western mountain slopes had been prospected clean. Some had returned to the east, many had died of their broken

dreams, and others lived on in California, too ashamed
to go home. With the end of the great Forty-Niner
Gold Rush, San Francisco had withered. Entire sec-
tions of the city had been abandoned and the rest
decimated by a series of hellish fires. There had been
no jobs, no money. The rich California agriculture of
early days which had flourished under the Spaniards
and, before them, the missionaries, had been too long
neglected.

Hunger had crouched over the Garden of Eden, but
fate had intervened. Almost exactly a decade after
Marshall's famous strike, the new discovery in Nevada
had been announced to the world and history repeated
itself. The stampede to riches was on.

Darby knew all of this because, as a western dime
novelist and historian, he'd been keenly interested in
such events. Today, Comstock silver fed this city and
injected new life's blood. Now, as he gazed about at
the prosperous banks, trading companies, hotels and
dealers of commerce, Darby realized that San Francisco was destined to become a great metropolis. It would
survive, even if the Comstock failed. The base of
industry was well-established. Elegant homes, permanent and solid, lined Telegraph Hill and told all who
came that San Francisco was going to outlast the
vagaries of mining. The city throbbed with pride and
optimism and Darby noted heady confidence in the
faces of its shopkeepers. Some day, he vowed, he
would return to this city when there was more time. A
story awaited his pen, but now there loomed more
immediate issues to resolve.

By the time he and Julia were settled in their rooms,
Darby knew the city was too big to physically locate
Suzette Trent. It might take months of searching and
endless questions. Much simpler, he thought, opening
the hotel copy of the San Francisco Chronicle, to place
an ad stating his purpose. After all, time was precious
indeed. Darby's advertisement was very simple.

*Mrs. Suzette Trent, For information on
location and health of your husband,*

Conrad, please contact Mr. Darby
Buckingham at the Parker House for
mutually beneficial details. Strictest
propriety and confidentiality on
the word of a gentleman.

Two days later, the woman arrived, sending a note of introduction from the hotel desk. He found Mrs. Trent nervously pacing the lobby.

Her daguerreotype had failed to capture her true beauty. Suzette's hair was black and hung in small ringlets about a heartshaped face. She was, Darby thought, a very pretty woman, though more petite than he favored. Dolly Beavers was far more lusty and healthful; she was built the way a woman ought to be. But Mrs. Trent made a striking appearance with her perfectly arched eyebrows and her porcelain-like skin.

"Mrs. Trent, thank you for answering our notice. This is Miss Bulette and my name is Darby Buckingham."

She nodded stiffly. Her dress was of excellent quality, though the writer's observant eyes told him it was overly used and, based on what he'd seen throughout the city, out of fashion.

"Your advertisement was specific enough and I will be equally so. Where is my husband and what is the state of his health?"

Darby motioned the woman toward a private settee. When they were all in place, he answered, "Your husband is in good health."

"Thank heaven," she said quietly and he saw her relax. "Is he still on that awful Comstock?"

Darby blinked with surprise. "You know?"

"Of course. Didn't he send you?"

Julia laughed and it wasn't an entirely nice sound. "He sent us, all right, but not as you might think."

Suzette Trent's eyes narrowed. "I don't know who you are, but I will leave at once if you in any way slander my dear husband."

Darby glanced once at Julia and saw the reflection of his own amazement. The woman was serious! Didn't she know there was another wife? No, of course not. This was a lady, though a troubled one. Darby decided to revise his original plans. One misstep and he felt certain the woman would refuse to help.

"Mrs. Trent, your husband needs you and there are many questions you no doubt have, but which only Conrad can answer."

He noticed Julia's smile but ignored it. "Can you return at once with us? It is very important."

Suzette Trent frowned. "I don't suppose he sent funds with you?"

Darby smiled. "Of course he did! I have them right here. Enough for trip expenses and some traveling clothes, should you need them."

Her reserve broke and she smiled. "I haven't seen my husband in almost five months. I have some very important news for him but . . . well, I think a man should learn in person that he's going to be a father, don't you?"

Darby felt as though he'd been shot between the eyes. Julia's hand flew to her mouth in shock. Blast the fates! Darby struggled valiantly to remain composed.

"I guess it doesn't show yet," she was saying. "I can hardly wait to tell him. We write, you know, but it isn't the same."

Her cheeks colored faintly. "I don't suppose Conrad would mind that I tell you this; he composes the most beautiful sonnets you've ever heard."

Darby coughed loudly and felt as though he'd swallowed a bone. First Dolly, now this poor pregnant creature. And, somewhere in the scoundrel's murky past, there was another wife who'd undoubtedly swooned over Trent's banal dribblings with unabashed rapture. Had the monster also provided the first Mrs. Trent with children? The possibility, the sheer outrageous possibility, made him tremble with outrage.

Later that night, as he lay in bed listening to the bustle of San Francisco, Darby sipped whiskey to calm his nerves. He tried to analyze just what it was about

Trent that woman found so irresistible. He worked the question over in his mind for a good half hour before giving up. Trent was a boor and a bigamist. He was a coward and a cheat who could not face defeat at the hands of a superior fighter. Yet, women . . . even seemingly intelligent women . . . were attracted by him! A mystery he would never fathom.

Mrs. Trent's devotion to her husband was an unexpected complication. He'd expected she would be hurt and vindictive enough to seize the opportunity to bring the philanderer down. He'd been wrong. Perhaps being pregnant caused a loss of blood from the brain? That might explain her loyalty in the face of infidelity. Or maybe . . . maybe she was in such dire finances that, with the coming child, she clung to the man out of monetary necessity. That seemed the most likely explanation. If that were the case, he would buy her help and thereby give her peace of mind. A favor for a favor. Money well-spent and for a good cause.

He fell asleep certain that he now had the answer. But, once in the night, he awoke from a dream in which Mrs. Trent had thrown the money into his face and actually helped Conrad. Darby decided he'd best wait until they arrived in Carson City before making offers. He never had understood the workings of the female mind—especially if it wasn't getting a sufficient blood supply.

On the mountain road, as they careened and slithered with heart-stopping frequency along precipices a thousand and more feet high, Darby revised his decision once again. From the moment they'd left San Francisco, Suzette Trent hadn't ceased talking about her husband and how proud he would be as a father. Darby knew she would never accept money for betraying the man she blindly loved. He was equally certain that Suzette wouldn't believe her husband was a bigamist and a confidence man.

Maybe Julia had reached the same conclusion because there was a tension in her even when the coach stopped to change horses. At the Genoa Station, they had a few moments alone.

"What are we going to do?" Julia asked. "You can't break her heart. She's so excited about the baby and telling him."

"Blast! Woman, I'd hoped *you'd* tell her."

"Absolutely not!"

"Then we'll have to stall," he said heavily.

"How?"

"I don't know. But it seems pretty clear that she must be prepared for the truth a bit at a time. That means we can't let her reach Virginia City."

"But . . . Darby! She's a free woman. We can't hold her against her will."

"Of course not," he said irritably, "we must appease the woman. Fabricate some convincing yarn."

"Good luck. That's your type of work, not mine."

"Thanks," he muttered as they climbed back into the coach.

Several hours later, Darby cleared his throat. "Mrs. Trent?"

She'd been abnormally quiet since leaving Carson City. It was as though she might be preparing herself for some uncertainty of the gravest importance.

"Yes?"

"Do you know what you husband does for a living?"

"He's a stockbroker. Although, I'm afraid, a very unsuccessful one."

"Ahhh, yes." Darby's face became serious. "Mrs. Trent, the time has come to admit that we have some rather disturbing news."

She blinked. Bit her lip. "Is . . . is he in danger? Is that why he didn't come himself? Please, be honest!"

"Yes. Yes, he is. Your husband is in very real danger of having his neck stretched. That's why we've come for you."

"Oh, no!"

She looked faint and he hopped across the seat, grateful there were no other passengers. "Mrs. Trent, would you rather I said no more until you are feeling better?"

"Go on," she breathed, "I am prepared for the worst. Has he been sentenced?"

"Not yet. In fact, he hasn't even been arrested."

She blinked, then recoiled from Darby as though he were a leper. "Then why are you trying to alarm me!"

"Because you're the only one who can help."

"Why should I believe you? Either of you? I'm beginning to think you're attempting to trick me into betraying poor Conrad."

"Betraying!" Darby roared. "Why . . ."

Julia intervened. "Woman to woman, let's be frank, Suzette. I'm sure that your husband has some very fine qualities, but every man has his weakness. Conrad Trent's happens to be greed and ambition. He's involved in a scheme to fleece the miners."

"That's not true!"

"Isn't it? Then why does he leave you alone in San Francisco?"

She turned away, and spoke in a small voice. "He said he thought it was better for me. That the Comstock isn't a decent place for a woman."

"Nonsense!" Julia snapped. "There are plenty of 'decent' woman in Virginia City. We're building a school, churches, and already have an opera house."

"You do?"

"Yes. The reason your husband wanted you to stay in San Francisco is because of his dealings."

The facade of disbelief slipped from Suzette Trent. "All right," she sighed, "I'll admit I've had my doubts. Conrad *is* too ambitious. A trifle egotistical, too, I suppose. He's . . . well . . . he's been in trouble before, though I'll never reveal the specifics. What can I do to help him this time?"

Darby's opinion of the woman soared. He actually smiled with warmth. "Your husband is involved in some kind of stock manipulation involving the Emerald Mine. Do you know anything about it?"

"No."

"It doesn't matter. He bought low and the stock went high. I am certain the mine is rich."

"He's smart," Suzette quipped. Now that the air had been cleared, the woman seemed at ease, with an entirely new personality. "Smart as a fox."

"Then *why* did he recently sell the stock? I mean, assuming the mine is worth a fortune."

"It isn't." She shrugged. "I can see by your expressions you don't believe that. But I know my Conrad. He neither buys nor sells unless he's certain of a stock's real value."

Darby scowled. Who could they believe? Young Patrick Cassidy was so certain.

"Mrs. Trent, I don't understand what your husband is doing. I know only that he's going to bring this whole mountain down on his shoulders. He may even be lynched before it's over."

"I won't let that happen, Mr. Buckingham! He is my husband. Tightfisted, it's true, but the father of my child. No matter what it takes. I'll stand behind him."

Darby nodded. He was seeing an entirely different woman than the one they'd found in San Francisco. He'd thought her nervous and fragile but it had been an illusion. Probably any apparent uncertainty had been her fear and suspicions regarding Conrad's activities.

"Mrs. Trent, I'm going to make an admission to you," he said. "You may not like me, or Julia, but it's got to be said."

"Then say it."

"When we came to find you, it was to destroy your husband. Discredit him and be the instrument of his downfall. Now, having met you and discovering that you are with child, we feel differently."

He waited for a response. She said nothing and he spat out the rest until there was no more to be told. "I would be content to see that no one gets financially hurt by his maneuvers and I'm sure he would get a very lenient prison sentence. I'd guarantee he doesn't hang."

"How generous," Suzette said icily. "And what am I to do in the meantime—beg?"

Darby leaned forward. "I'll hire the best lawyer I can to represent your husband and I'll see you and the baby are financially supported until the prison sentence is over."

She gazed out the window for a long time. Her eyes glistened and she dabbed them dry. "Very well. How can I help?"

"Stay away from your husband until we're certain how he intends to profit. After that, I'll bring him to you before we hand him over to the Federal Marshal in Carson City. He'll be safe there."

"Unharmed, Mr. Buckingham. Not a mark on him."

Darby's lips tightened under his bristling moustache. Trent *owed* him a rematch.

"Whatever you're thinking, Mr. Buckingham, you'd better change it. Those are my terms and, if you won't accept them, I'll go straight to Conrad with the warning. I would anyway except for my condition and there will be no more running. This baby I'm carrying will turn him into an honest family man."

"I agree to your terms but not your opinion. The man is no damned good."

"That's my problem!"

Darby hit off a harsh reply. "The last town before we reach Virginia City is coming up. I'll see you're comfortably situated in the Gold Hill Hotel."

"I can't pay for it."

"I wouldn't allow you to," Darby mumbled.

She reached out and touched his sleeve. "You've been paying for all of this, haven't you? The clothes, the steamboat to Sacramento, and the stage coach."

He was too embarrassed to admit the fact.

"You don't have to answer. I knew it from the beginning. You're not a very good liar, Mr. Buckingham. In the future, you should avoid it if at all possible."

"Blast!" Darby swore. Then he lapsed into brooding silence.

It was long after dark when Julia and Darby walked over the Divide that separated Gold Hill from Virginia City. There were few travelers on the road and, below, the campfires danced like fireflies while, above, stars winked back at them. They moved hand in hand, and Darby felt that Julia was troubled and filled with sadness.

She led him to her door and, for a moment, they stood listening to the early evening bustle of the mining town—laughter, the tinkle of an old melody played on an out-of-tune piano.

"Want to come inside?"

"I can't."

She nodded. "I know. There's nothing for us. You'll go back to Dolly. That's what this whole thing was about anyway."

"Julia . . ."

"Don't say it," she warned. "If you're not coming inside now, you never will."

"We can be good friends," he argued, hating himself because it was such a nothing offer.

"Sure we can." Her head lifted. "You'd better go. It's not late and I'll have some business."

"Dammit, Julia! Why don't you pack up and return to San Francisco? Find that respectable husband you talked about."

She laughed. A harsh, cutting sound. "I believe I just did, Mr. Buckingham. Fairy tale hour is passed. Goodnight."

Before he could stop her, Julia was through the door and gone.

He walked a block down the street and halted to light a cigar. Something held him and he knew it was Julia's parting and that there wasn't a damned thing he could change about any of it. Perhaps a half hour later, he hadn't moved. The cigar was almost gone. Then, he saw Julia emerge from her doorway, reach up and illuminate a red lamp, then go inside.

Darby shook his head and felt very old. He pitched his cigar to the dirt and savagely ground it under his heel. Then, he walked away.

Three Cuban cigars glowed in the dark room overlooking C Street. Darby, Zack, and Bear stood by the window and patiently waited.

"What time is it?" Darby growled.

"Almost midnight, I reckon."

"Then where the hell is she!"

"Take it easy, Darby. Miss Beavers hasn't stayed the night with him yet. I told you Zack and I been keeping a watch on 'em. Most every night it's the Silver Crystal Club. Sometimes an opree. If he'd have driven her to his house, we'd have been there waiting."

Darby shifted impatiently, his nerves wire-tight. He'd found Zack and Bear, now all that remained was seeing Dolly again. And, in the back of his mind, he was very worried. Could she have fallen in love with the man? God only knew. She might even hate him for exposing Trent and bringing the man's wife to the Comstock. That was a risk he had to take. If Dolly was in love with the bigamist, he could save her from losing her money and pride, but nothing he could say would ever heal the wounds between them.

Zack spoke up. "We thought you was dead or gone. It's a good thing you came back tonight, 'cause tomorrow is our big payday."

"What do you mean?"

"I mean Trent's machinery arrived this morning and tomorrow he gets his loan. Eighty thousand dollars. The man is going to buy back all the Emerald stock. Twenty bucks a share."

"What!" Darby spun around. He could barely see Zack. "There's whiskey in the cabinet. Maybe you'd better update me on a couple of facts."

"Maybe I had," Zack said dryly. "Most everyone in Virginia City with Emerald stock is going to be lining up at Trent's office at sunup. Even Dolly. He talked her into it the last few days. Bear and me see it different. We don't know nothing about stocks, but this whole thing seems like a rigged deck."

Darby slammed his hand down on the old buffalo hunter's shoulder. If Conrad Trent was buying up the stock, it all became instantly clear. Patrick Cassidy *had* been right from the beginning. He never should have doubted the boy's mining assessment.

"Zack, you and Bear may not know stocks, but you can smell a skunk when no one else can."

"Huh?"

"Never mind. I'll explain when Dolly arrives. Where ..." His words rattled still as the familiar carriage and team of sorrel horses pranced onto C Street.

They waited for Dolly to emerge from the coach. It was clear she was having some difficulty saying good night. The door was open and, once, Dolly's shapely ankle was half out but disappeared back inside again.

"Blast! I'll kill him!"

They caught him at the door and, somehow, the pair made him stay in the room while they went down to settle the matter. Darby lurched back to the window and saw them appear almost immediately. Conrad and Dolly must have too, because Dolly came flying out of the coach and there was a shouted order to the driver to apply the whip. No more prancing, the four horses bolted as Zack and Bear slammed the door shut.

He could hear Dolly arguing. Her voice was angry and upset. But at whom? And for what?

Darby turned away from the window and strode over to the liquor cabinet. He didn't waste time pouring; he drank it straight. As soon as Dolly came into the room, he'd know where he stood with her. Know if Conrad Trent had stolen her heart away. Know ...

"Darby! Oh, Darby!" she screamed. And then she was in his arms, tasting his kiss, holding him as though there was no tomorrow.

Over her shoulders, Darby saw the two old buffalo hunters in the doorway fidgeting uncomfortably. Behind Dolly's back, he crooked his forefinger to motion them in. There was a lot of planning to do before Conrad Trent opened for business and there wasn't much time. Not enough, even, to close the door and be alone with Dolly and tell her the things he should have said from the beginning.

From the way she was kissing him, Darby knew he was making a real sacrifice.

ELEVEN

It was eight forty-five and, in fifteen minutes, the Nevada Bank of Commerce would open its door for Conrad Trent. His eighty thousand dollars was ready and there was a line in front of his office that had been forming since daylight. They'd take what the stockbroker would pay as long as his money held out—and they were grateful for the offer.

Darby Buckingham rose early and trudged past the collection of stockholders; they acted like sheep lined up to be fleeced—they were in for a surprise. He nodded at a couple of familiar faces and walked up C Street until he turned and reached the bank on B Street. There, he posted himself as inconspicuously as he could and settled to wait. He lit a cigar and absently fiddled with the derringer in his pocket, hoping he wouldn't have to use it. Time crawled and he kept checking his pocket watch, feeling the tension build up inside. Over and over, he reviewed the plan and still he wasn't satisfied. Conrad Trent was neither a fool nor a coward—anything could happen. The man was quick with his gun and, if shooting erupted in front of the Nevada Commerce Bank, someone might get killed.

Darby snapped his watch shut with authority. There was no use worrying any longer. The plan was set and the time was at hand. Any moment, Conrad would appear and nothing could change the course of events to follow. His watch read nine o'clock.

Bear was ready. Darby saw him a half-block away, perched quietly on the driver's seat of a buckboard. He was pretending to wait for Tucker's General Store to open so he could load. Darby was encouraged by the amount of freight traffic which had built up during the past hour. The more wagons, the better. Everything was going to depend on surprise and confusion so, if the streets were jammed, it was to their advantage.

A line of tall-sided ore wagons rumbled onto B Street. Whips cracked and the mules strained in their harnesses. The wagons bore the sign of the Kentucky Mine Company and Darby saw they were loaded high with rock, probably on their way to a stamping mill down by the Carson River.

Suddenly, Zack Woolsey rode into view and gave the signal. Darby's hand reached inside his coat pocket and he gripped the derringer, feeling sweat on his palm. Then he saw Conrad Trent carrying a satchel, and beside him was Dolly Beavers. They looked for all the world as though they were taking a pleasant morning's stroll. He heard Dolly laugh gaily and watched Conrad lean over to whisper something that made them both smile. Darby shook his head with appreciation. The woman had nerve. She was completely ignoring the big, shambling bodyguard who walked only a few paces behind. Darby studied the stranger intently. The guard seemed relaxed and his gunhand wasn't poised in readiness. Maybe Dolly's laughter had disarmed the man's caution. The trio entered the bank and the door closed behind them.

In front of Tucker's General Store, Bear Timberly sat up straight and gathered the lines in his big fist. Zack Woolsey prodded a sorrel horse toward the bank and Darby headed across the street. The windows were only partially shuttered and he glanced inside. Dolly and the bodyguard waited as Trent stuffed money into the satchel under the inspection of Mr. Croft. They were almost finished. Darby swung away from the window and signaled to Bear and Zack. Both came down the street from opposite directions. Slow and easy—they attracted no attention at all.

Trent fastened the satchel and shook hands with the banker. Then, offering his arm to Dolly Beavers, they headed for the door with the bodyguard following closely.

Outside, Darby waited with his back pressed up against the wall. When they stepped into the morning sunshine, his derringer cocked ominously.

"Don't move!" he warned. "Don't even make a sound."

Dolly grabbed for the satchel but, for an instant, she shielded the guard. Darby saw the man's shoulder dip for his gun. There was no time to push Dolly aside and strike. Darby looped his gunhand up and smashed it into the man's jaw. He collapsed without a whimper.

Everything seemed to happen at once. Trent wrenched the satchel away from Dolly and pivoted to run. Bear's whip cracked and the buckboard jumped forward to slam Trent into a hitching rail. Darby was on him before the man could stagger to his feet.

He grabbed Trent by the nape of his neck and hurled him against the wagon. "Get in!"

"Go to hell!"

Trent filled his lungs to shout for help and Darby drove his shoulder into the man's ribs. The warning cry came out a painful gasp.

"Gawddammit," Bear raged, "get him in this wagon and let's roll!"

"I'm trying!" Darby grunted as he picked up Trent and threw him into the wagonbed.

Darby ripped a tarpaulin over them and the satchel came flying into his face. It hurt. "Thanks, Dolly. Now create your diversion!"

They were fortunate. The line of wagons blocked the opposite side of the street and, though it seemed everything had gone wrong, all the foot traffic was down on C Street expecting Trent's momentary arrival.

All except Allen Walker.

Darby saw him bolt out of a doorway. There was a gun in his hand and a bullet seared the air over the wagon.

"I'll kill him. Let him alone. I want to kill him!"

Both he and Trent looked up and, as the wagon

jolted into motion, another bullet split the morning air.

"Who's that!"

Trent ducked under the tarp. "A crazy bank clerk. Get us out of here!"

They were finally starting to roll. Allen Walker was firing his gun and screaming like a wild banshee. Dolly Beavers ran in behind him and Darby saw her purse lift in the air and come crashing down on his head. The man batted her away and came sprinting after them.

He was gaining!

"Bear! For God's sake, move this thing!" Darby shouted as a bullet splintered wood just inches from his face.

"I'm trying! These freight wagons got us boxed in!"

Their pursuer had a clean shot into the open buckboard. He was now less than twenty yards behind. The man stopped, seemed to gain control. For the first time, Darby saw him really take aim and so he poked his derringer out and squeezed the trigger, knowing he'd miss. The range was too great and the wagon's jolting made his arm bounce violently.

The derringer and the six-gun barked at each other. A bullet plucked the tarp and slapped into wood.

Zack Woolsey flashed into view like a knight in armor. The animal he rode was obviously one of Trent's lumbering sorrel carriage horses. The sorrel could have pulled a cannon, but it had no speed. Zack urged it forward. He was dressed in Conrad Trent's suit and a new Stetson was pulled low over his eyes. Both men were tall, the clothes fit perfectly, and Darby marveled at the deception. Zack had even forsaken his buffalo rifle for a six-gun.

He opened fire on Walker and, at the same instant, unleashed a blood-curdling Comanche war cry. Their pursuer was completely unnerved. He ran, with Zack hot after him. It was a sight worth remembering. Zack spurred the sorrel right up onto the boardwalk and the hooves clattered after the runner. Walker was fast and the horse slow, but Zack finally managed to overtake his quarry a block away. His stirrup kicked up and knocked his man spinning into the closed doorway of Zellenback's Saddlery. Walker bounced a good six feet before he landed in a pile.

Zack reined back into the street and fired his gun into the air. "So long, Rubes. Thanks for the eighty thousand!"

He unstrapped paper-stuffed saddlebags and whirled them overhead, then sank spurs and managed to get the carriage horse into a high gallop on the road north. All in all, it was one hell of a fine performance.

Someone opened fire from the doorway of a butcher shop and Dolly began to yell.

"Help! Help! Trent is getting away with our money. Someone stop him!"

"He won't get ten miles!" Trent cursed as they watched a stream of people come pouring in from C Street yelling to mount a posse.

"They'll never find him," Darby growled. "As soon as he's out of town, he'll rip that suit of yours off and be in buckskins. Then he'll bury the clothes and the saddlebags and turn your horse free. He's a mountain man, Trent. That counts for something. Bet on it!"

As they neared the end of B Street and rounded a corner, Darby saw a dozen horsemen flying off like the U.S. Cavalry. They'd reacted faster than Darby had expected. And that big, lumbering carriage horse wasn't going far. Yet, Zack would have at least a mile's jump on them and that should be enough to insure Conrad Trent would become the most wanted man in Nevada.

He felt good. In spite of every imaginable foul-up, they'd escaped and no one had been killed by accident. "Just like one of my dime novels," Darby told the man beside him. "Who knows? We may have just immortalized you."

"What's that supposed to mean? If you think that fiasco is going . . ."

"It'll work. You still don't get it. We've made you an outlaw, Trent. As far as the people of Virginia City

are concerned, you stole eighty thousand dollars of
their money. They'll be furious enough to post a big
reward; it will read dead or alive."

"You're crazy, Buckingham!"

"Am I? Do you really think they'd believe you
again? Dolly told me about your great performance. It
wouldn't work a second time. Not without the eighty
thousand."

"My guard will tell everyone what really happened,"
Trent said stubbornly.

"With your reputation, he'll probably think you set
him up. Maybe he'll even try to collect the reward—
that would be the smart thing to do. No," Darby said
quietly, "those people have to blame someone and *you*
are the prime candidate. Besides, who are they going
to trust? Another of your hirelings, or someone like
Dolly Beavers?"

"You've thought this all out. Just like one of your
hack plots, well . . ."

Darby grabbed him by the throat. "I promised I'd
not leave a mark on your face. But nothing was said
about the neck down. Your wife . . ."

Trent recoiled as if Darby had tossed him a rattlesnake. His eyes bulged and his lips formed silent
words. He grabbed Darby by the shirt-front and whispered. "Suzette?"

Darby pressed his gun to the man's chest. "Before
doing something fatal, you'd better let go of me."

"You brought Suzette over here!"

"That's right. We're going to see her now. She's
waiting for us at the Gold Hill Hotel. Getting you
inside without attracting attention is my next problem.
We go in by the rear staircase."

Trent released his grip and sagged in defeat. "So
that's where you and Julia went."

"Uh-huh."

Bear reached back and yanked the tarp. "Line of
wagons coming up. Pull this over and quit jawin'."

It was dark underneath and, just to make certain the
stockbroker didn't try anything foolish, Darby pressed
his gun into the man.

"Go ahead and shoot, Buckingham. I don't want to face my wife anyway. Not like this. Not with the choice of a rope or dying an old man in prison."

"You should have thought about it sooner."

"Yeah. But I underestimated your hatred and over-estimated your sense of fairness. I never would have thought you'd stoop so low as to drag a woman like Suzette into this."

The words stung as Darby listened to the wagons roll past. Bringing Mrs. Trent over wasn't a thing of which he was proud. There just hadn't been a better way. When the crunching wheels faded in the distance, he yanked the tarp aside and glared at this accuser. "Your wife is a fine woman, mister. But then, I'm not an expert on women—that's your specialty."

Trent's face went crimson except for his lips, which were tight and bloodless.

"Listen," Darby spat angrily, "from the day I arrived in Virginia City, you've been a man without honor or remorse. You cheated the Cassidys, killed one and chased the other away, you challenged me to a fight and won on a foul, you're a bigamist yet you tried to seduce my woman, then you put Julia and me in that mine shaft to die. If killing you would help, I'd gladly do it with my bare hands."

Trent smiled coldly. "Noble speech, Buckingham. But you've got a few things wrong. Don't forget that I tried to befriend you, only to receive insults in my own house."

"Your poetry *is* tripe!"

"Obviously, there are those who would disagree. Furthermore, I profit from the greed of others. If that makes me a swindler, then I'll plead guilty; but I never robbed a poor man or took another's wife. And I'm no murderer."

"Tell that to Patrick Cassidy," Darby gritted. "He doesn't laugh much these days."

"You were there!" Trent raged. "I didn't come flying out of my coach hoping to spill blood. He gave me no choice. Quinn went crazy and I shot him in self defense. I could have killed Patrick at the same time, but I didn't. In your case I just *had* to win. There is no other way for me."

Darby started to tell him he'd better get used to another way but Trent couldn't stop.

"As for Miss Beavers, I can only say I was as helpless under her charms as you had to be when you made the decision to drag my wife into this mess. And killing you and Julia wasn't *my* plan. I had to survive, and your burglary gave me no alternative. You couldn't be bought and you had me in a corner. I recall warning you about that the first time we met. Roan was a killer. He died of a broken neck by your hands. Look to yourself!"

"I have, and my conscience is clear. You are a slick man with words. Too slick. No matter what you say, the fact remains that you're a bigamist. Tell me, does your first wife love you as much as the second poor woman?"

"Yes. Yes, she did."

"What do you mean 'did'?"

"She's gone. My first wife is dead."

"What!"

Trent's face went bleak and wintery. "She died in childbirth aboard a ship named *The Challenge*. We were storm-driven for two weeks rounding the Horn. Winds as hard and cutting as razors. Seas as high as pines. She . . . she never told me when we left Boston she was expecting. If so, I'd have stayed back East."

His voice became a tortured whisper. "I . . . I loved her. She kept me honest."

"I don't believe you," Darby said quietly.

Trent didn't seem to care. "We were going to a new land—a new chance. We both wanted a son. Caroline died and the doctor on board said our child was a boy. I went crazy. Insane. Suzette was a passenger and . . . and she kept me from leaping into Chilean waters."

"Blast! And so, you infected her with your own misery and took her for your wife."

"Something like that, yes."

"Without love?"

Trent groaned. "She *knew* how I felt. I made no promises. I didn't care. *She* did! Even knowing I'd never forget. Ask her, Buckingham!"

He didn't need to ask. Trent was an actor and a liar, but no one could deny the misery written on his face. And it made sense that, in his drunken moments, Trent would talk about his first wife. Anguish drove him into the admission and it even explained why Suzette would abide his failings.

Darby looked away. None of this changed things, but at least he now pictured the devils which twisted their forks into Conrad Trent's mind. Could the man be salvaged? Was it even worth trying? Maybe so. A wife and infant son buried at sea might very well crack anyone. The loss was so tragic that Darby couldn't even think about how he would have reacted.

He sighed. "Trent, I have some news for you. Suzette is carrying your child."

"No!" Trent clawed for his throat like a demon whose last thread of reason had snapped, hurling him down into a chasm of black insanity.

It took all of Darby's great strength and weight to subdue him and he might not have succeeded even then if Bear hadn't set the brake and jumped over the seat to help.

"You bastard!" Trent raged, "I'll swing from a rope never knowing my child!"

Bear raised his huge fist. "Let me put him out of his misery."

"No!" Darby stared into Trent's pain-filled eyes. "I won't let you swing. That's a promise."

"Then I'll rot in the State Penitentiary. No thanks. I'd rather be *dead* than watch my wife and child age through prison bars. See their pain, and live in shame. If that's your idea of mercy, then I've one suggestion."

"What?"

Trent punched himself in the chest with his forefinger. "Put your gun right there and make it count."

Darby shook his head. "How much farther, Bear?"

"Not far," Bear said, lowering his fist and climbing back into the driver's seat.

Darby nodded. "You'll live to see your child." It was all he could say and even that was a promise he might not be capable of delivering.

They had to wait almost an hour until Darby was certain there was no one about to see them. During that time, Bear decided to go for some refreshment while Darby and Trent lay under the tarp. The air was stifling. There was no conversation between them, but Darby had plenty of time to ponder the fate of the man at his side. It was feasible that he might suggest a way to have Trent's prison sentence shortened for the welfare of Suzette and her baby. But that was up to a judge. All he could do was to petition for leniency.

Darby peeked out. He couldn't see anyone. "Let's go. Just remember, if you're recognized, there's nothing I can say to prevent a hanging."

Trent nodded stiffly.

The dash up the stairway was accomplished without incident. Even the hallway was vacant. Darby stopped at Suzette's door and tapped.

"Who is it?"

"Buckingham. Open up."

The door swung open and she flew into Trent's arms crying. It was all Darby could do to get them inside and the door closed. He stood to one side of the room, his eyes averted.

"Ahh, my dear. How I've missed you! My love for you runs as deep and pure as the great silver veins beneath our feet. It's as broad as the Sierra skies and as sunlit and fresh as snow on the high mountain passes."

Darby's eyes rolled and he wished for a drink.

"Oh, Conrad. Just to hold you. To hear your voice, to . . ."

"Please, hush, my darling. For I bring sadness with me. But you . . . you bring life."

Suzette moaned. "Then you know."

"Know! My heart, it is the only reason I allowed

Buckingham to deliver me here. Were it not for our child, I . . . I'd rather have died than face you this way. I am lost!"

Darby chewed his moustache in his vexation. This reunion was like witnessing a bad play!

"What is to become of us, Conrad?"

"You must go. Alone."

"No!"

"You must!" Trent said passionately. "I can face anything except the thought of you and the child sharing my fate. I am doomed!"

There was a long moment of silence, then Suzette, her voice firm and cold, said, "You are *not* doomed. I will save you."

The finality of those words made Darby pivot. The gun was aimed at his heart. The woman gripped it with both hands and said, "If it is a choice between you and Conrad, as God is my witness, I will not hesitate to fire."

When he looked into those frightened eyes, they reminded him of trapped animals. He knew without the slightest doubt that she meant every word.

Conrad Trent took the gun from his wife's shaking hand. "I believe I can handle things now, my love. You have given me life."

Darby felt a chill go up his spine. From the expression on Trent's face, he guessed *his* life was very close to ending.

TWELVE

"What were you going to do with me?" Trent asked quietly.

"I don't know. That depended on what Bear, Zack, and Dolly proposed."

Trent waved his gun with an air of dismissal. "I'm not interested in them. What would *you* have wanted? Secondly, what were your intentions concerning that satchel of money? Eighty thousand dollars, Buckingham. Even for a man of your means, that is rich temptation."

"I'd have returned every penny," Darby said stoutly. "The only reason we took it was to prevent you from buying the Emerald stock. We know it's valuable."

"How?"

"Something your dear wife remarked."

Trent looked toward Suzette who was staring in her clenched hands.

"Love?"

She glanced up at Darby. "He won't kill you, Mr. Buckingham. My husband isn't a murderer. I could not love a murderer nor have one for the father of my child."

Trent swung away sharply, a troubled frown creased his brow.

Darby looked straight at them. "He also told me that he wasn't a killer. Mrs. Trent, I almost believed it too."

"Quiet!" Conrad lowered the gun a fraction. "If you'd have given the money back to the bank, everyone would have lost. The stockholders and myself. There has to be a better way."

"Sure," Darby offered cryptically. "You're going to kill me, take the money, and run."

"Conrad . . ." Suzette touched his cheek.

He drew her close. "I won't leave you with child, and I won't have you running in fear at my side."

Darby lowered his hands. "Perhaps there *is* a better way. A way in which we can undo most of the harm."

"Impossible."

"Conrad! Please, listen to him."

"All right, but it's hopeless for me."

Darby didn't wait for the man to change his mind. "I'll make this short. You and I both know the only way out of this is to go back down to the Emerald Mine and dig until we hit ore."

Trent scoffed him. "Brilliant! We might not touch silver in a month of digging."

"We could try."

"By hand? The machinery I bought will be impounded! We'd have to use picks. You have no idea of the physical punishment required even on one eight-hour shift."

"I'm equal to it," Darby challenged. "Are you?"

"Certainly! But you forget Virginia City will be wild for my blood. I'd be shot as soon as I crossed the Divide."

"We'll get you in the same way we got you out. And, once inside the mine, we'll keep people away." Darby's chewed up moustache bristled. "Dammit, man! I've nothing to gain! I'm offering you a chance. If we *can* strike silver, you'll be almost forgiven. You'll be sentenced to a few years in prison rather than being lynched or having a bounty hunter track you down. For eighty thousand dollars, there are men who would follow you to the ends of the earth!"

Trent expelled a deep breath. "It's not much of a chance, my love. What do you think? I could go to South America. Wire you money and . . ."

"No, no, no! Conrad, I've never asked you to do anything until now, but if you try this, even if you fail, people will know you were repentant. Your child will grow to understand. You won't remain in prison forever."

He shook his head and studied each of them for a long time. Then, his broad shoulders lifted and he, without saying a word, pitched the gun to Darby Buckingham.

Bear Timberly eased inside. The buffalo rifle dangled from the crook of his arm. Bear spat a stream of tobacco juice back into the hallway.

"Trent, I reckon you made the right decision—for onc't," he drawled.

Later that afternoon, Dolly Beavers arrived. Upon learning that Darby and Trent were to go into the Emerald Mine, she shook Conrad's hand. "You'll find it. I know you will."

"Sure," Trent said without conviction. "Just . . . look, no matter what happens, promise me someone will take care of Suzette."

They all nodded.

Zack Woolsey appeared just after dark, swearing that being chased by a posse was more fun than he'd had in years. His only regret was that Trent's horse was too damned slow to entirely circle Sun Mountain.

It was time to leave and Darby once more outlined the plan. Bear and Zack were to work a claim next to the Emerald Mine on property owned by Conrad Trent. He drafted a mining release and dated it so that there'd be no trouble. The idea was to sidetrack any intruders who might try and rework the Emerald, a remote possibility, given the circumstances of Roan's death. At night, they would take turns at watch beside the Emerald Mine and relay messages and provisions as needed to Darby and Conrad working below.

Dolly and Suzette were to figure out a way to anonymously return the eighty thousand dollars.

As they were leaving, Suzette Trent motioned Darby aside. "I know how you feel about Conrad. But please watch out for him. Give him a chance."

Darby nodded. "When he handed your gun over, he made his own chance. Just wish us luck."

Outside, the air was cold and the heavens bright. Darby filled his lungs with clean air and tried not to think about going back down that mine shaft. If they succeeded, everyone would win—young Patrick, his family in Ireland, and the Virginia City miners who'd spent their hard-fought earnings on the dream of making enough money to live on when their arms and backs were too stiff to wield a hammer, their hands too broken to hold a drill.

He nodded to everyone. "We are going to find silver. Nothing can stop us now."

"Freeze or I'll shoot!"

Darby pivoted. In the moonlight, he saw them. The crazy one who'd opened fire on B Street and another man who held a gun as if he knew how.

"Hello, Leroy," Trent said, in a hushed voice, "I didn't expect to see you again."

"First honest words I ever heard from you. Guess everyone knows this here is Allen Walker. Seems almost like a family get-together this evening. Conrad, I think I'd better take your gun first."

"Come and get it."

"Uh-uh. I know you too well. Walker, step up and relieve Mr. Trent of his temptation." Leroy smiled. "You sure pulled a slick one on the town. Would have worked too, if Walker and I hadn't compared notes. Your rear left wagon rim is coming off the wheel. Made it damned easy to follow the track."

He stepped up to Darby and poked his gun into the writer's throat. "Enough talk. Where's the eighty thousand?"

Darby kept his hands at his side. He couldn't move them fast enough to stop a point-blank bullet. "In the hotel safe," he finally said.

The gun barrel jammed into flesh and Darby wanted to choke.

"Don't try that line! You and Conrad had this thing planned from the very beginning. I won't be fooled a second time. Now, while you still have a neck, where is the eighty thousand dollars?"

"It's under the tarp!" Dolly exclaimed.

"Walker, check it out. If it ain't there, I'll pull the trigger." He glanced sideways. "You grab Trent's gun?"

"No, but I thought you wanted me to . . ."

"His gun first!"

"Under my coat," Trent hissed.

Walker was shaking and his gun danced. With his free hand, he reached inside Trent's coat. The stock-broker's hands blurred in motion as he swatted the gun off-target. A bullet wanged off rock and Trent grabbed Allen Walker.

Leroy swore. He jerked back and snapped off two quick bullets at Trent who held Walker pinioned like a shield. The bank teller arched his spine as lead drove into his body. He rose on the balls of his feet and pranced like a puppet.

Darby threw himself at Leroy and knocked him spinning to the ground. The gunman rolled and came up in firing position.

That's when a buffalo rifle kicked him skidding back three feet in the dirt. He convulsed and fired another bullet into his own leg. He didn't feel a thing.

Trent released Allen Walker's body and opened his arms for Suzette. He gazed at Darby. "You remember what I did when my trial comes. It ought to count for something."

Darby nodded in agreement. His throat still ached from the gunbarrel's pressure. "I'd say it does," he graveled. "Now, let's get out of here before everyone in Gold Hill comes to investigate."

For Darby Buckingham it was like being forced to return to his grave. His every instinct cried out in protest as he lowered himself into the Emerald Mine shaft. The blackness assailed his spirit and he felt the heat reaching up from the depths to drag him down and suck the very strength from his arms.

As he went deeper, the walls seemed to lean in on him from above until, like a trapdoor, they slammed shut and left him dangling over eternity.

As soon as his feet crunched rock, Darby struck a match and waited until tools and provisions were lowered by rope; then, to keep his mind from reliving circumstances, he grabbed a pick and set to work.

After several minutes, it became apparent that it was too cramped for both of them to safely handle picks, so they alternated. In less than an hour, they were each bathed in sweat and bare to the waist.

Blisters formed at once, but neither man paid them any heed until they popped and made the wooden handles slippery. They ripped their shirts and wrapped the handles. Neither would slacken the pace, nor stop for rest—even as the shirt wrappings stained crimson.

The rock was as hard as iron and unyielding, but both continued the attack. They'd begun by throwing their corded strength at the floor three hundred times before changing places; the rate tumbled each hour until neither could swing more than fifty times at a stretch. Muscles cramped, lungs burned for air, and the heat made them stagger with dizziness.

Finally, they rested until Trent lurched up and grabbed the pick. He was so weak he had to almost manhandle it to his shoulder.

"It's my turn," Darby said.

"Yeah, but it's my life in the balance," Trent grunted as he drove the blade into the hole.

Darby nodded and let the man go but, when his own turn followed, he wouldn't quit until he doubled the count. Whether stated or not, they were engaged in a contest of strength and will. Neither man intended to lose. Hour by hour, the pit deepened until the rest of the floor became a mound of rock shards.

"We have to get this rock out," Darby said.

Trent grinned. "I thought you'd think of some excuse to call a halt."

The remark was so ludicrous that Darby took no offense. "You're out on your feet."

"So are you."

"What time is it?"

"One o'clock."

"Is that all?" Darby asked. "Seems like we've been down here longer."

Trent pointed upward. There was no dot of sunlight. "This is our *second* day."

Darby nodded and called until Zack answered. Minutes later, a bucket filled with meat, bread, and a canteen was lowered. In its place they sent up rock to be scattered above. They had the floor cleared before dawn and were swinging the picks again. Darby judged they'd gone nearly twenty feet. It didn't seem like very much—not when measured by pain.

Time lost meaning. Only depth was real. Each man moved like a rusted machine, worn and battered beyond its work life. Between swings, they dozed in fitful intervals. They reached a point where just getting the pick above the shoulder seemed nearly impossible.

Darby wasn't certain what was different, yet, almost in a stupor, he realized something *had* changed. He rolled his head like a punch-drunk fighter and stared over at Conrad who was asleep.

"Trent." No answer. "Trent!"

The man pushed himself up on one elbow. "Is it my turn again?"

Darby snorted. Trent didn't realize it, but he'd been out for more than two hours.

"It's the rock," Darby wheezed. "It's gone softer. I can feel it in my arms. And the sound, it no longer rings."

Trent blinked, scrubbed his fatigue-lined face before coming over to inspect the rock. When he held it up to the candle, all his sagging weariness vanished.

"Well!" Darby asked expectantly. "Well?"

"I'm not sure, but I think it's time we got us an assay report."

The pick slipped from Darby's bloody hands and he crumpled. "It *has* to be silver. I'm nearly worn out."

Trent actually snickered. "It's age, Buckingham. You can't whip a younger man."

Darby remained motionless but his voice quivered a passionate warning. "We'll soon find out, Trent. And that's a promise."

"Yeah. It won't take the assayer long. I'll send it up now."

"You do that." The fact that Trent had misunderstood the threat bothered the writer not in the least. A time of reckoning was almost at hand.

The candle flickered low as the two exhausted men lay prostrate against opposite rock walls.

"If the ore is high grade, what are you planning to do with me?"

Darby frowned. "I'll tell the judge how you tried to redeem yourself."

"That's not much. In fact, it's damn little."

"What else *can* I do? You made your own troubles."

"And I've already paid for them. Every dollar I took went into macinery. The Emerald stockholders will make a fortune. I'll leave the Comstock penniless."

"Not quite. You've still got Patrick Cassidy's twenty-five percent plus some very valuable mining properties. Also ill-gotten, I suppose."

Trent smirked. "You don't remember so well, do you? We had a bet and you lost the fight."

"We both know what happened," Darby growled. "I would have finished you." He stood heavily. "I'll have that Emerald Mine stock of Patrick's."

"Not without another bet," Trent vowed, pushing himself erect. "If you win, I'll gladly turn it over. If I win, you let me take Suzette and go free."

Cold satisfaction made Darby bellow, "I accept!" He raised his fists and moved forward. His bull-neck, never much more than a truck extension of his sloping shoulders, melted into his body. Wild, blood-pumping excitement filled his veins as they began to circle.

Trent stayed out of reach. "Watch out for that left hand, Buckingham. Use it on my jaw and it'll shatter those fingers. Leave you crippled. It hasn't . . ."

He jabbed Darby hard in the face twice and danced away.

"It hasn't healed," he continued. "Not completely."

Darby brushed a trickle of blood from his lip and smiled. "You're right."

And with that, Darby feigned a looping overhand that Trent ducked easily. His eyes were glued on the right and Darby let him watch it as he lashed a vicious left uppercut to Trent's exposed ribs. Bone cracked— rib bones. The collegiate boxing champion slammed off the rock wall and doubled up with pain. He grabbed his side and swayed gasping in pain.

"You lose the bet," Darby said, backing away.

"No! I never lose. Can't lose! My wife and child *need* me!"

"You're finished. Beaten!"

Conrad looked up and raised both fists. "You'll have to kill me before I quit," he coughed, lurching forward.

Darby waited, his expression deeply troubled. This was courage. A rare display and totally unexpected. He lifted his hands and, when Trent moaned, trying to swing, Darby's fist drove in and cracked against the jawbone. Trent's eyes went blank and he crashed to the rock floor and rolled to a stop, face down.

The writer turned him over. Trent was out cold. "As I said," Darby whispered, "I'll have Patrick Cassidy's stock. And . . . and you did lose."

Darby sat on a pile of rubble and quietly smoked his cigar until the shout from above told him the news they'd all wanted to hear. Dolly, Bear, Zack, and Suzette were yelling down at them from the opening above, yet he didn't hear them as he stared at the motionless form nearby.

When his Cuban cigar was properly smoked down, he threw it away and decided to leave. Never again would he descend a mine shaft. He grabbed the rope and started up. His arms felt weak from the long brutal hours he'd worked them and his lips tasted blood from Trent's fists.

At the top, Dolly, Zack, and Bear were in a state of

wild exhilaration and kept repeating something about twenty-two hundred dollars per ton. He smiled and pretended to act excited, but the detached presence of Suzette clouded his spirit. She was studying him, trying to smile, but failing miserably. Darby knew what she wanted—her husband, the father of her child.

He started forward. There was a stiff, clean wind and it pressed her clothes to her body. Darby could see the outline of the life she carried.

"Mrs. Trent, there's going to be a huge celebration tomorrow when we announce the discovery."

She nodded. "I'm glad. I . . . I don't feel much like celebrating myself, but . . ."

Suzette started to duck away and a muffled sob escaped.

He grabbed her. Pulled the woman close and spoke for all to hear. "Dear Mrs. Trent, your husband probably wouldn't object to missing tomorrow's festivities either. May I suggest that tonight you both depart the Comstock?"

Suzette's lovely face uplifted and tears streamed down her cheeks, though she radiated wonder. She threw her arms around Darby's neck and began to kiss him over and over.

Darby finally glanced across at Dolly Beavers. She understood. Dolly was smiling and crying, too.

AUTHOR'S NOTE

During the seven years I lived in Carson City, the Comstock Lode was only a few miles away and beckoned like the painted lady she always was. Back in the 1860's, she really glittered and her promises of fortune lured the best miners in the world to her bosom. For those she favored, and who were tough and smart enough to play her, the lady was lavish. Like Conrad Trent in *Silver Shot*, the men who profited most were the mine owners and stock manipulators such as Flood, Fair, O'Brien, Mackay. Irishmen all, they became known as the Silver Kings and were each worth between ten and twenty-five million dollars. Of the four, James Flood was probably the shrewdest in circulating rumors and manipulating stock prices to his advantage. Conrad Trent would have been green with envy over Flood's "milking machine," as it was dubbed by unhappy speculators, and which netted him some fifty million dollars in only three years!

But for each Comstock millionaire, there were thousands who came and went away poorer, and many others who died hundreds of feet into the steamy catacombs under Sun Mountain.

I've been down some of those shafts and tunnels, felt the air grow hot and oppressive, known the sensation of rock walls pressing in all around. I believe the old hard-rock miners were as tough a breed as ever labored in the west. Up in Virginia City, in the long saloons such as the famous Bucket of Blood, you can sip a beer and gaze at their pictures, note the grim purpose in their faces and the muscles which ridged their rock-bustin' arms. And looking out toward the hell-gone-forever of Eastern Nevada, you can see the cemeteries on the hill with their sharp white crosses and little picket fences. They didn't bury Julia Bulette with the townsfolk. She has her own resting place because, even then, folks knew she was a special kind of woman and she was honored, just as she told it to Darby Buckingham. One cold winter day in 1867 Julia was found strangled for her jewelry, and the population of Virginia City gave her one of the most impressive funerals in Nevada history. The entire Comstock shut down and hundreds of miners, led by the volunteer fire companies and the Metropolitan Brass Band, wept openly as Julia was lowered to the strains of *The Girl I Left Behind Me.*

Through its rich and exciting history, the Comstock Lode yielded at least $500,000,000 in silver and an equal amount in gold. But at last it played out until even Dan De Quill, outstanding editor of the *Territorial Enterprise* and close friend of Mark Twain, finally departed vowing the Comstock would again rise to prominence. And after all those years, Dan never regretted spending his career in Virginia City because it throbbed with life and excitement.

Today, I'll admit the old lady is old and beaten. Her boards are cracked and in need of paint and, though it's been over a hundred years, her hillsides are still denuded and covered with abandoned mine tailings. Yet, in the quietest seasons of the year, when the hills are dusted with fresh snow, you can hike in solitude and almost feel her—still alive, still calling.

At least that's how I feel whenever I return to the Comstock. And, like Dan De Quill, I have a hunch the lady isn't through yet. There are new mining companies buying up the old abandoned claims and starting back into production. It'll be different this time around, but even the big new machines won't really change the way of things. Men will still have to go down into the earth and, for those with enough grit and daring, the rewards and dangers will be the same as they were a century ago. And when all the roar and dust fades away, when some have died and some gotten rich, the lady will still be there, a little more wrinkled, but still waiting for the next dance.

Darby Buckingham may return to Virginia City and Dolly Beavers. Right now I'm just not sure because there's an entire West alive with stories he has to chronicle. Big things were happening. Like the struggle of the Central Pacific Railroad to bust its way over the wild and mighty Sierra Nevadas. I don't see how a man like Darby could resist such a story that was taking place only a few hundred miles away. The fact of the matter is, he couldn't as you'll discover in the next Derby Man adventure, EXPLOSION AT DONNER PASS.

—*Gary McCarthy*

Watch for the next Derby Man adventure

EXPLOSION AT DONNER PASS

It's the Derby Man to the rescue when the Central Pacific Railroad challenges the towering Sierras and a mysterious wave of terrorism threatens every hard-won foot of track. The workers' tempers are seething, the winter snows are mounting and suddenly, trapped like the members of that ill-fated wagon train years before, Darby must conquer Donner Pass or die.

A Bantam Book available June 1st wherever paperbacks are sold.

And don't miss the Derby Man in

THE PONY EXPRESS WAR

Look sharp, hit hard—that's the Derby Man's style. He's a fast-moving mountain of muscle who throws himself into the thick of the West's greatest adventures—like the Pony Express, a grueling 2,000 mile race through hell. The pace and terrain are deadly enough but vengeful Paiute warriors and murdering saboteurs led by a sadistic giant threaten to turn the route into a trail of blood. Until one man has the brains and brawn and guts to save the Pony Express —the Derby Man.

This Derby Man adventure is now available wherever Bantam Books are sold.

LUKE SHORT
BEST-SELLING WESTERN WRITER

Luke Short's name on a book guarantees fast-action stories and color-ful characters which mean slam-bang reading as in these Bantam editions:

☐ 13679	CORONER CREEK	$1.75
☐ 13585	DONOVAN'S GUN	$1.75
☐ 12380	SILVER ROCK	$1.50
☐ 14176	FEUD AT SINGLE SHOT	$1.75
☐ 14181	PAPER SHERIFF	$1.75
☐ 13834	RIDE THE MAN DOWN	$1.75
☐ 13838	TROUBLE COUNTRY	$1.75
☐ 13760	DESERT CROSSING	$1.75
☐ 12634	VENGEANCE VALLEY	$1.50
☐ 12385	THE SOME-DAY COUNTRY	$1.50

Buy them at your local bookstore or use this handy coupon for ordering:

BANTAM'S #1
ALL-TIME BESTSELLING AUTHOR
AMERICA'S FAVORITE WESTERN WRITER

- [ ] 13561 **THE STRONG SHALL LIVE** $1.95
- [ ] 12354 **BENDIGO SHAFTER** $2.25
- [ ] 13881 **THE KEY-LOCK MAN** $1.95
- [ ] 13719 **RADIGAN** $1.95
- [ ] 13609 **WAR PARTY** $1.95
- [ ] 13882 **KIOWA TRAIL** $1.95
- [ ] 13683 **THE BURNING HILLS** $1.95
- [ ] 14013 **SHALAKO** $1.95
- [ ] 13680 **KILRONE** $1.95
- [ ] 13794 **THE RIDER OF LOST CREEK** $1.95
- [ ] 13798 **CALLAGHEN** $1.95
- [ ] 14114 **THE QUICK AND THE DEAD** $1.95
- [ ] 14219 **OVER ON THE DRY SIDE** $1.95
- [ ] 13722 **DOWN THE LONG HILLS** $1.95
- [ ] 14316 **WESTWARD THE TIDE** $1.95
- [ ] 14227 **KID RODELO** $1.95
- [ ] 14104 **BROKEN GUN** $1.95
- [ ] 13898 **WHERE THE LONG GRASS BLOWS** $1.95
- [ ] 14411 **HOW THE WEST WAS WON** $1.95

Buy them at your local bookstore or use this
handy coupon for ordering: